Cinderella
Liberty

Cat Johnson

CHAPTER ONE

Camp Leatherneck/Bastion
Helmand Province, Afghanistan
August 2013

The night sky lit with the glowing red trails of incoming fire. It was like the Fourth of July back home, but a hell of a lot less fun.

Instead of being in a tank top and shorts, kicking back in a folding chair with a cold beer in his hand and seventeen more in the cooler, Crash was hunkered down behind a berm with the grit of Afghan dirt between his teeth.

The noise of the incoming rockets was deafening. Meanwhile, as crazy as it seemed, his attention kept straying to how the rocks beneath him were jabbing into his legs through his uniform. That was when he wasn't occupied wondering if any deadly scorpions or black widow spiders were lurking nearby. God, how he hated anything with more than four legs.

The butt of the M4 semi-automatic rifle pressed into Crash's shoulder as his jaw clenched with determination. He had no intention of dying today as Gunnery Sergeant John O'Malley. He was going to live long enough to be selected for Master Sergeant, and after that, Master Guns, and these bastard insurgents weren't going to be the ones to take that away from him.

He'd survived a float to Iraq, plus two deployments to Djibouti and he hadn't seen any shit like this. Yeah, at Camp Lemonier there'd been a vehicle-born IED that luckily never made it to the front gate, but there were no frigging rockets.

Crash was an aviation mechanic. He was an air-winger, not an infantryman. His MOS didn't normally put him in the line of direct—or hell, even indirect fire during ground combat like this. The closest thing he had come to being shot at was the twenty-eight days of Marine Combat Training at Camp Geiger when he'd first come in, and those shots were blanks.

He'd be damned if he'd get killed during the drawdown, when the US was in the process of pulling out of this godforsaken country and turning the running of it over to the Afghan military.

"What the fuck!" Zippy was next to him, lying facedown like Crash, manning his own weapon. "These bastards have some big frigging balls."

Crash had to agree. To attack an installation this size took some major *cajones*.

Camp Bastion was the main British military base

in Afghanistan, as well as the air hub used by the US Marines. Adjacent was Camp Leatherneck, NATO's headquarters for the region. Between the two, there was a good amount of firepower stationed here.

That didn't seem to matter to these crazy motherfuckers lobbing shit at them. No, it seemed as if their Southwest Asia enemy, Taliban-Charlie, was not going to make this deployment easy.

"Command knew this was coming," Crash shouted over the noise.

They had to have known. Too many orders had come down the pike recently, changes to procedure, all of which pointed to preparation for a suspected attack.

At least this time the camp had been prepared. Unlike last September when a small group of Taliban dressed in stolen US uniforms waltzed right onto the base one night thanks to cutbacks in security and patrols. That mistake had cost the good guys a few refueling stations, half a dozen hangers, eight Harriers and, far more devastating than the material losses, the lives of two US Marines.

For once it seemed the military had learned from past mistakes. This time, personnel had been issued extra ammo and told to sleep with their weapons within reach. Extra foot patrols had been added, no one was allowed to travel to the other side of camp after dark, and they'd been told not to gather in large groups, which included eating in the chow hall.

That last order had been the most inconvenient. Take-out food was fine at home when Crash could grab something to go from the window of a fast food joint and bring it back to the barracks. Here? Not so much. But for safety's sake, all the new orders were necessary. For once command had made a change for a good reason instead of their usual arbitrary, bullshit rules.

Obviously, the big brass had taken whatever chatter they'd heard on the lines seriously. They'd been correct, right down to the timing of the attack—the end of Ramadan when the Muslim world celebrated the completion of a month of daytime fasting with a feast.

Crash had searched online and read all about the religious observance that had provided them with a month of relative peace on base. But judging by this attack, the opposition had taken their *Lailut ul-Qadr*, Night of Power, to mean something totally different than their religion dictated. The enemy was marking this holy date with a show of strength against the coalition troops, and they'd done it with a bang—literally.

Well, Crash had some power of his own. He gripped his weapon a little tighter. He was a damn good shot, but they'd been issued a limited number of rounds. Every shot had to count. And bullets wouldn't do much good against mortars or rockets anyway. The bad guys were flinging all sorts of shit at them over the chain link perimeter fence topped with razor wire.

It didn't matter. If Crash went down, he'd go down fighting, but he wanted it to be with a clear conscious. There was something he needed to get off his chest.

"Zip, I gotta tell you something."

Over the sound of the incoming fire, Zippy must have heard the gravity in Crash's tone. "Jesus, Crash. We're not gonna die here today so keep your damn confessions for another time. All right?"

"Just listen, please. I need this off my chest."

Zippy let out a huge breath. "Okay, go ahead, but I'm just gonna mock you with whatever you tell me later when we're back home having beers."

Crash sincerely doubted that. He launched into his confession anyway. "In May, while we were in New York, I slept with your sister."

For the first time since they'd taken position, Zippy took his eyes off the perimeter. His gaze cut to Crash, just for a second, before it moved back to the fence. "We're both gonna survive this, so that afterward, I can kick your ass."

From Zippy's mouth to God's ears…

CHAPTER TWO

Marine Corps Air Station New River
Jacksonville, North Carolina
Three months earlier...

"We're meeting the boat in Morehead City the day after tomorrow to head up to New York for a few days. Then we're taking the bird back to New River." Crash sat at his desk, office phone in hand for his weekly phone call to his mother.

"I thought it was supposed to be called a ship, not a boat."

Crash grinned. "Yeah, technically it is. Marines call it a boat just to tick off the Navy guys. They hate it." Just one of the many pleasures of being a Marine.

His mother giggled and he smiled wider. It was good to hear her laugh. Since his father had died, he'd worried more about being apart from her than usual.

The Marine Corps Air Station in North Carolina wasn't incredibly far from where his mom now lived in Florida, but too far to visit as often as she'd like him to. So for now, until he put in his twenty years and retired, a phone call and the few times a year he got to see her would have to do. Then again, if the promotions he expected came through in a timely fashion, he might just go to thirty years. Nothing was set in stone. Such was life in the military.

"It sounds like a nice trip. New York should be fun. Take lots of pictures for me, but be careful, John. Promise me."

"Yes, Mom." Crash smiled.

His mother would have been equally excited and worried for his safety no matter where this trip took him. The war zone. Disneyland. Wouldn't matter to her. She'd be happy he was happy, and then she'd worry. That was what mothers did, he supposed.

Crash, on the other hand, was genuinely excited. He'd never been to New York. This detachment would be a hell of a good time. The perfect pre-deployment trip for the whole squadron before they left for Camp Bastion.

Afghanistan. Hell of a place to spend the next seven or so months…and he couldn't freakin' wait.

He'd never been there either and he wanted that damn Afghanistan campaign medal before he retired. With the troop drawdown in that region and less and less units being deployed there, it had been iffy for a while if he'd get to go at all.

But the orders came and he was going, though

not until after this detachment to the Big Apple.

"Gunnery Sergeant O'Malley—" A Marine who looked young enough to be fresh out of boot camp in spite of his stripes stopped dead in the open doorway when he saw that Crash was on the phone.

He held up one finger to the kid who was making him feel every one of his thirty-something years just from his presence in the office. "I gotta go. I'll call you soon, okay?"

"Okay, baby. Stay safe."

"Yes, ma'am." He rolled his eyes at her never ending concern for him and replaced the receiver on the cradle of the desk phone. "Yes, Corporal. What can I do for you?"

"Gunny Zipkin asked that you meet him at the Officers Club at sixteen-thirty."

"Oh, did he? And why didn't he call me?"

"His cell phone, uh, took a swim." The kid's lips twitched as he said it, as if he was trying to contain a smile.

Crash ventured an educated guess at what had happened. "He drop it in the toilet again?"

"That's correct, Gunnery Sergeant," the young Marine responded with a barely hidden grin.

"Well, that explains that." With a snort of a laugh at Zippy's idiocy, Crash glanced at the time in the corner of his computer screen.

Half an hour of his workday left to go. He'd planned to go back to his quarters, do laundry and pack for this det. Now it appeared as if he wouldn't be heading directly to the staff barracks after work today. "Did he happen to mention why he needs me to meet him at the O Club?"

"He mentioned a tactical planning session."

Crash hid a smile. "A'ight. Thank you."

Dismissed, the Corporal left Crash to his thoughts. He knew very well what Zippy's tactical planning sessions entailed, especially when they were held at an establishment that served alcohol. Drinking. And while they did that, no doubt they'd be making a plan for more drinking in the near future. Most likely Zippy wanted to discuss logistics for their off-hours in New York.

They'd man the rails as they pulled into port, and have a few official duties—VIP tours of the boat, some party with the big brass—but after that their time was their own. The first night they were free until zero-seven-hundred the next morning. Their last night there they only had until midnight before they'd have to be back on the boat. Good old Cinderella liberty. You would think that a grown man who was a careerist could be trusted on his own home turf to make it back aboard the boat prior to the commencement of any duties, not have a curfew at midnight like a teenager, but such was life in the Corps.

That was fine. They could get into all sorts of mischief about town during that off time. As long as they were checked back in and on that boat by twenty-four hundred hours, it was all good. *That* kind of boat det he could handle.

He wasn't even pissed they'd be in uniform the entire time, even while on liberty. Nothing worked as efficiently to attract the ladies. That had been proven time and time again in real world experience. There was good reason Marines called their uniforms *Superman clothes*, and it wasn't because it gave them the ability to fly. It did, however, often give them the ability to see beneath women's clothing.

New York City. Women. Two nights of freedom. It sounded like a hell of a good time to him.

Glancing at the time again, he realized he'd daydreamed away the end of his day. Good thing he'd gotten all his work done early so it didn't matter that he was goofing off now. Frontloading, getting the needed work done as fast as possible, was something he'd been taught during his first days in a squadron. It was the best way to enjoy more FOT—fuck off time.

He stood and ran his hand over his closely cropped hair before planting his cover on his head. He'd have to get a haircut before they left for this det so he didn't start to look shaggy by the end of the trip. Weekly haircuts, no matter what. So it had been since he'd joined. So it would be until he retired.

Maybe he'd grow his hair out after that. Probably wouldn't go with the mullet that had been so popular when he'd joined, but he'd keep it longer than it was now. It never got long enough nowadays to tell for sure, but he feared he had a whole lot less hair than he used to. Sad but true, but that's what the years will do to a man. He had nothing close to the amount he had when he'd first sat in that chair at Paris Island and the barber buzzed off what had been a nice thick head of dark blonde waves.

The ladies who used to be jealous of Crash's hair in high school would no doubt hardly recognize him now. The hair may be questionable, but at least he still had the blue eyes the girls used to swoon over back in the day. Though there weren't a whole lot of swooning women lately, time couldn't take those from him.

It was a short drive from his office at the squadron to the O Club, which was walking, and sometimes stumbling distance from his barracks. He could have walked if he'd wanted to, but it was hot as hell today. Why walk when he could drive in the air conditioning? Not too long from now he'd be sweltering in Afghanistan so he might as well take advantage of whatever moderate luxuries he had here on base, driving privileges included.

Crash parked his car in the nearly empty lot of the Officer's Club. The place was never crowded unless there was a party being held there. It could be because only officers and senior staff NCOs were allowed to go there. It could be because it was only open Wednesday through Friday and closed at nineteen-hundred, which was pretty damn ridiculous. More likely it was because the places off-base, just outside the gate, were a lot more fun. Particularly the ones that featured poles...and dancers wrapped around those poles.

Nope. No strippers here at the O Club, but at least there was a pool table and sometimes strategically placed vats of hot chicken wings and fresh popcorn.

Lack of scantily clad females aside, the Officers Club at New River was pretty nice. The coolest part was the bar area. Squadrons from on base donated different pieces of memorabilia to dress up the place. Tail rotor blades, murals, mugs and the like lined the walls and the shelves behind the bar.

Crash didn't care what it was that kept other Marines away. All that mattered to him was that it was close by, the beer was cold and fairly cheap, and he could walk home if he needed to. It was a winning combination for him.

For his buddy too, apparently. Zippy had arrived enough ahead of Crash that he'd had time to get himself a beer already.

Crash walked up behind him and laid a hand on the man's shoulder. "You know, if you didn't insist on playing that stupid ass word game on your cell while taking a crap, you might not have to go get yourself another phone."

Zippy twisted on the bar stool to glare at Crash. "Just because you can't spell for shit doesn't mean *Words with Friends* is stupid, and that's not how it happened anyway."

"Oh? This was a new and different phone toilet mishap? Do tell." Crash dragged a stool from beneath the bar and propped his ass on it.

"No. It doesn't matter. Forget about it. Just order yourself something." He frowned and became overly interested in the label on his beer bottle.

Zippy avoiding the question so vehemently had Crash intrigued. "Well, damn. Now I have to know."

"No. Drop it." Scowling, Zippy raised the bottle and chugged.

"Come on. What? Tell me. Were you looking at porn while snapping your bean over the bowl and dropped—" He'd meant it as a joke, but Zippy sputtering on his mouthful of beer had Crash halting mid-sentence. "Oh my God. That's it? Is that what happened?"

"Shh." Still coughing into his fist, Zippy glanced behind him, no doubt to see where the bartender was. Probably concerned because for this particular shift the bar was manned, as it were, by a female.

Crash was close to busting a gut laughing, but he managed to contain himself. Mostly. He couldn't believe they were having this conversation at the O Club, but it was just too good to let go. "Oh, man. That is too funny."

Zippy turned back, frowning. "As if you've never done it."

"Held my phone in one hand to look at dirty pictures and jerked off into the toilet with the other? No. I haven't."

"Shh!" Zippy shushed Crash again. "Jesus, Crash. Not so loud."

To keep the man from blowing an artery, Crash leaned forward and kept his voice low as he said, "How about using your imagination, Zip? Or, I don't know, look at it once then put the damn phone down somewhere safe."

"Can we let this drop now, please?"

Crash ignored that request as a horrifying realization hit him. He'd borrowed Zip's phone. Not too long ago, actually. He'd had that damn thing pressed right up against his face.

"Shit." Crash shook his head. This situation was definitely less funny after that memory. "I'm gonna remember to never ever touch your phone ever again. Jesus, God only knows what's on—"

"I'll have another one and he'll have the same. Thanks." Zippy talked right over Crash as the bartender neared their end of the bar.

She turned to get their beers from the cooler and Zippy spun on Crash. "Can we please talk about our plans for New York instead of this?"

"Sure, let's talk about New York. So while we're on the boat, are you planning to watch some porn and snap in the dark in your rack with all the rest of the squadron right there, or you gonna hog the head so you can do it in private?"

Zippy narrowed his eyes and shot Crash a less than friendly look. "Just for that, I'm not gonna tell you my news."

"Aw, I'm heartbroken." Luckily for Crash and his broken heart, his beer arrived. He grabbed the bottle, dripping with icy condensation, and took a sip, letting the cold foam wash down his throat.

Definitely worth stopping in for the ice cold beer alone. The fun of torturing his friend was just a bonus.

"Fine. I won't tell you that my sister Trish and her hot friend Dawn are meeting us in New York while we're there."

Now it was Crash's turn to narrow his eyes at Zippy. "Hot friend? Zip, this better not be a fix-up."

"No, of course not. You want to be alone. Be alone. I don't give a shit. Don't mean I can't have a nice visit with my sister before we deploy."

"Your sister *and* her friend. Why is she bringing a friend if she's there to visit you?"

"Because I don't want her wandering around that friggin' city alone, that's why."

"Okay." Crash had a sister of his own so he couldn't argue the point. Zippy was a New Jersey native, not a born and bred Southerner like Crash, but a man's instinct to protect his sister was universal. Still didn't mean he trusted Zippy in this situation. The man had been trying to play matchmaker for him for a month now. "But I swear, Zip, if I think you're trying to hook me up—"

"I know. I know. You'll find your own damn woman when you're ready." Zippy lifted his beer and mumbled behind the bottle, "*if* you're ever ready."

Why couldn't his friends understand his situation? Finding out the girl you'd been dating had been running around on you was enough to turn a man off relationships for a good long while.

"Give me a damn break, Zip. It's only been a few months." Crash didn't think that was an excessive amount of time to take to recover. And it wasn't as if he hadn't gone out and had a few flings to soothe his male ego after that particularly devastating blow.

"Whatever. I didn't say you had to date Dawn. Just be nice to the girl so my sister doesn't feel bad for bringing her—" Zippy stopped. "Aw, crap."

"What?" Crash hated to ask, because it probably wouldn't be good.

"I was supposed to call Trish today to firm up plans." Zippy blew out a breath. "I'll have to stop by the office on the way home and use my desk phone. I called to get a new cell overnighted to me so I'd have it for the det, but it won't be here until tomorrow."

And so they'd gone full circle, back to the sunken phone. Happy Zippy's attention had moved away from Crash's sorely lacking personal life and on to something else, he slid his cell across the bar. "You can use my phone. Just don't take it into the bathroom."

Zippy reached out and grabbed it. "Ha, ha. Funny man."

"I think so." Crash grinned. "You remember her number, butter fingers?"

"Yes, of course I remember her number." Zippy screwed up his mouth and shot Crash a look. "She's my sister, you dork."

Crash shrugged. "Just asking. A man who hasn't learned after drowning not one but two phones in the shitter over the past six months might be a little challenged in the uh, area of mental capacity."

"Whatever." Zippy pressed the phone to his ear. "Be quiet. It's ringing."

While Zippy waited for his sister to answer, Crash took another sip of beer. He was starting to get excited about the det again.

It would still be a hell of a fun time up north. Zip and his sister might very well be up to no good and playing matchmaker, but not even that could ruin this trip.

He just had to get through his workday tomorrow and then he'd be on his way. New York City had better watch out.

CHAPTER THREE

New York City

"Trish, I'm so, so sorry I couldn't come with you today. Are you sure you're okay there in the city all alone?"

"I'm fine, Dawn. Really. I've been to Manhattan by myself before. And my brother should be here any minute." Trish glanced at the clock in the dashboard of her car.

"I still feel bad."

"Well, don't. I'll just have to have fun with all the hot Marines on my own." Trish smiled as she heard Dawn's groan through the cell phone.

"Don't remind me. I can't believe I'm missing Fleet Week for jury duty."

"You're doing your civic duty." While Trish would be doing hers here in New York by supporting the troops—or at least ogling them. Her gaze tracked two sailors as they crossed the street. Well worth the hour and a half drive from home. Seeing her brother would be nice too.

Dawn sighed. "That won't be much comfort while I'm sitting there bored to death in some courtroom and you're surrounded by hundreds of men in uniform."

"I think it's more like thousands of men in uniform, actually."

"Great. Rub it in some more, thanks. Crap. They're calling us back into the courtroom. I'll call and check in later. Text me if anything good happens. Oh, and send me a picture of some hot military guys so I have something to look at."

"Yes, ma'am. Talk to you later." Trish disconnected the call.

It definitely would have been much more fun if Dawn had been able to come but at least she'd have her brother, Danny.

Her phone buzzed and she glanced down to see his name on the readout. Speak of the devil...

She hit the button to answer. "I see you replaced your cell so you don't have to call me from your friend's phone anymore."

"Yes, I did. And no teasing. I've had enough from him on that subject. Where are you?" he asked.

"Where you told me to be. Parked along the curb in front of your ship, and hoping the cops don't chase me since I've been here for like twenty minutes already and this is a no parking zone."

"I know. Sorry. They just cut us loose now. We'll be right down."

"Okay. See ya."

We. Trish had to wonder who Danny had with him. She supposed she'd find out soon enough.

He wasn't right down as he'd promised, but about ten nerve wracking minutes later, as Trish kept one eye trained for parking enforcement and the police because she'd been standing in a no parking zone for half an hour, her brother and one other guy appeared. A very large guy, she noticed. One who filled out his uniform quite nicely.

"Hey, Trish. Good to see you." Danny hugged her, and then peered past her into the car. He frowned. "Wait. Where's Dawn?"

Danny's obvious disappointment had Trish laughing. "She couldn't make it. And it's very nice to see you too, big brother."

"I thought you were bringing her."

"I thought I was too, but something came up." She gave up waiting for her brother to make the introductions and turned to the Marine standing off to the side. She extended her hand toward him and couldn't help but notice he had the bluest eyes she'd seen on anyone, male or female, in a long time. "Hi. I'm Trish."

"Sorry." Danny turned to include his friend in the conversation. "This is John O'Malley, but you can call him Crash. We all do. Crash, this is my sister, Trish."

"Nice to meet you, ma'am." He took a step forward and extended one arm toward her.

She smothered the urge to cringe at the *ma'am* and chose instead to focus on an inventory of his assets. He was tall, just like she liked in a man and big, with nice thick arms and large, strong hands. The kind that would make a woman feel truly held. She couldn't see his hair beneath his hat, but that didn't matter. A man with a jawline that strong would look good no matter what. In a short military haircut. Hell, even bald.

And that uniform... Very nice. Sure, her brother was dressed in the same thing, but somehow it didn't look quite the same. This Crash certainly filled out his well.

His large hand wrapped around her smaller one, much like his smooth southern drawl seemed to envelope her, making her want to hear more. She managed to say, "Nice to meet you too. Danny's talked about you before."

"Has he?" His sandy brows rose above eyes the color of the summer sky. "Forgive me if that worries me a bit."

As he released her hand, Trish laughed. "Don't worry. Nothing bad."

He shot Danny a look, and then focused his gaze back on her. "I'll have to trust you on that."

Danny rolled his eyes. "Don't worry about Crash. He's always suspicious of me. So where do you guys want to go first?" He rubbed his hands together and looked from one to the other.

"We've both been here a bunch of times, so maybe we should ask your friend what he wants to do." She turned to Crash and wondered how he'd gotten the nickname. They called her brother Zippy, but since their last name was Zipkin, that was a no-brainer. But John O'Malley being called Crash? Must be a story there somewhere and she hoped to find out what it was before the night was over.

Crash shrugged. "This is my first time so everything's new to me."

He was so adorable she'd gladly take him anywhere he wanted. "My hotel room is near Times Square." She glanced at her brother. "We could park my car there and walk most places, I guess."

"As long as there's booze and women involved, I'm fine with it."

Trish rolled her eyes. "I don't think that's what Crash wants to do on his first trip here."

"Are you kidding? That's exactly what he wants to do. We're leaving for Afghanistan where we can't partake of either of those things." Danny reached for the passenger side door handle. "Come on. Let's go. Times a wastin'."

"All right." Trish sighed. She'd take her pain in the ass brother to a bar, but it would be by way of some tourist attractions so Crash would at least see something while he was here. "Why don't you let your friend sit up front so he can see better?"

Danny's brow creased in a deep frown. "No. I need to be up front so I can tell you where to go."

"I know where to go. We're only driving to the hotel and the damn streets are numbered, Danny. How lost could I get?"

Crash moved toward the back of the car. "It's fine. I can see plenty from the back."

"See?" Danny cocked a brow. "Just get in."

"Fine." Trish noticed the smirk on Crash's face as he opened the rear door. Apparently sibling bickering amused him. That was a good thing. Trish had a feeling he was going to see a lot of it today.

She managed to get to her hotel and park the car without killing her brother and his incessant back-seat driving, even if it was from the front passenger seat, but it left her good and ready for that bar Danny was so intent on getting to.

They'd just hit the sidewalk and she was considering options when Danny started to look antsy. "Where we headed?"

"How about we walk to Rosie O'Grady's for drinks? It's not too far." And they'd pass lots of cool places along the way.

"Sure. That'll work." Danny agreed and Trish hid a smile.

She'd managed to get her way so Crash could see some sights. The iconic lights of Times Square. A few of the Broadway theaters. And the walk would take them right past the famous Military Island where the Armed Forces Recruiting Station was. Though come to think of it, Crash might not be as excited about that as Trish always was as she tried to get a glimpse of some men in uniform.

It didn't matter. Just the crowds and people watching in the city, and particularly in Times Square, were worth taking the time. There was certainly a lot to see already, and they'd just arrived. A horse across the street caught her eye. She put a hand on Crash's forearm to get his attention, but all it did was capture hers—those were some rock hard muscles the man had.

He glanced down at her to see why she'd stopped them.

"Look." Trish tipped her head toward the officer on the horse standing right in the middle of the sidewalk on the other side of the street.

Crash followed her gaze and she watched as his eyes widened. "Holy... A cop on a horse. Right on a New York City street."

"What's the hold up?" Danny had finally realized they weren't behind him anymore and backtracked to where they stood.

"I was showing Crash the policeman on horseback."

Danny glanced across the street. "And?"

"And, maybe he'd like to get a picture taken with him."

Crash's eyes got brighter. "Would he let me?"

"We can ask." Trish shrugged.

"Okay, I'll ask. Will you take it?" Crash pulled out his cell.

"Of course, I will." She took the phone and eyed the scene across the street. The massive animal with the officer atop his back. The neon behind him. Crash in uniform. It would make one hell of a photo. "Run on over and I'll take it from here so I can get a wide shot."

"A'ight." Crash grinned like a kid who'd just heard the ice cream truck turning on to his street. He waited for a yellow cab to creep by, and then trotted across the road.

Next to Trish, Danny stood shaking his head. "Look at him. He looks like a damn tourist."

"He *is* a tourist. Leave him alone. He's having fun." Trish smiled as she watched Crash crane his neck, looking up to talk to the officer seated so far above him. She glanced back at Danny. "If you run over there, I'll take one with the both of you."

Watching Crash, Danny pulled his mouth to the side like it was a ridiculous suggestion, but then he rolled his eyes. "All right. I guess it might look kind of cool since we're both in our Charlies."

Trish laughed. "In your what?"

"That's what we call this uniform. Just take the picture and don't worry about it." Danny turned toward the street and made his way across, dodging the traffic.

She may not know the names of all of the Marine uniforms, and until now she hadn't much cared, but she wasn't opposed to learning. Especially if Crash was her teacher and the body tucked away beneath his Charlies was anything like she imagined.

Trish raised the phone, hit the camera function button and lined up the shot. The two Marines in their short-sleeved khaki shirts and green trousers with their chests decorated with ribbons earned over the years made for an impressive sight, one that had a few passers-by taking a second look.

Smiling, she snapped the picture and planned their next stop, which would not be Rosy O'Grady's if Trish had any say in it. Oh, they'd end up there, but *after* Crash got to see more of the city.

Trish did a good job of it. Before they finally pushed through the front door of their final destination over half an hour later, she'd managed to cram in a few more things, including Crash's first New York City hot dog and pretzel from a street vendor.

Inside the cooler air of the dimly lit restaurant, Danny bypassed the main level and led them down the stairs to the bar. He aimed for an empty table.

"What do you want to drink? I'm buying."

"Thanks, Zip." Crash dipped his head in a nod. "Beer for me."

"Yeah. Me too." A nice cold beer sounded good after walking around the hot city.

"Okay. Be right back." Danny headed for the long bar against the right hand wall while Crash pulled out two chairs from where'd they'd been tucked beneath the table. One for Trish and one for himself.

"Thanks." A man who pulled out chairs for a woman. Where the hell had he come from? With a smile on her face she couldn't control, she decided to ask. "Where are you from, Crash?"

Certainly not New Jersey. Sure, Trish was used to having men pump her gas, but only because that was the law in her home state. This whole chivalry thing was new to her, but she could easily get used to.

"Alabama originally. Now I'm in North Carolina with Zip and my mama is in Florida."

Trish nodded. That explained so much. The soft drawl she heard in his voice. The manners she didn't come across too often in Jersey men, her brother included. "Well, then I'm glad I got to show you a little bit of the city."

"Me too." Crash glanced at the bar then leaned forward a bit. "You know, I think Zippy was upset your friend couldn't come. He was fixin' to hook me up with her."

Trish swallowed away the bitter taste of disappointment. Didn't that figure? The guy she had the hots for was already hot for her friend. She needed to find new girlfriends. Maybe some old, married ones. "Did you want to be fixed up with her?"

"Hell, no." He sounded pretty adamant and, bitchy though it might be, Trish was happy he wasn't interested in something with Dawn. "I'm glad she didn't come. I mean, no offense to your friend. I don't even know her and I'm sure she's real nice, but I don't need a fix up. I'll find my own women, when and if that time comes."

"No offense taken. I totally understand." Trish's mind reeled with all the information Crash had just spilled. He didn't have a girlfriend, but from the sound of some of the comments, she wasn't sure he wanted one.

"Besides, it would be crazy starting something up now with us leaving for Afghanistan so soon." He shrugged.

Trish nodded. She knew Danny was deploying. Now she knew Crash was part of the unit going with him. No wonder he wasn't interested in a relationship. "Yeah, you should enjoy yourself. Just have fun. Don't worry about anything serious."

What the hell was she saying? Since when did she believe in not getting serious and just having fun? Ever since turning thirty a few months ago, Trish hadn't looked at a guy without sizing up his marriage potential. What she'd said to Crash was the opposite of her usual philosophy.

The question was, had she meant it?

Thinking about it, Trish realized she might mean it. Given a choice between a one or even a two-night stand with the blue-eyed hottie before her, or nothing at all, she'd take the fling. She was sure it would include some great sex and provide memories that would hold her for a long time to come.

The ringing of Trish's cell phone in her purse broke into her naughty thoughts. That was probably a good thing, though finding the phone in her purse was a challenge. Finally, her hand connected with it. She pulled the cell out and saw the display read *Dawn*.

Crap. With a glance toward Crash, Trish touched the button to answer. "Hey, Dawn. We were just talking about you."

Crash's brows rose at the mention of the name.

"Good things, I hope." Dawn laughed.

"Of course. What's up? How's jury duty?"

"Excellent."

Dawn's answer surprised Trish. "Excellent? I thought you were miserable."

"Oh, I was, which is why it's extra good that I've been released from duty. I'm in the car and on the road, on my way to you now."

"You're what?"

"I'm coming there. The minute they let me go I ran home, grabbed an overnight bag and got in the car. If I don't hit traffic, I'm hoping to meet you there in an hour."

"Wow, that's great. Call when you hit the city." Trish eyed Crash again. She guessed she'd see soon how opposed he really was to this set-up her damn brother had planned.

"Oh, I will. Get those military men warmed up for me. I'll be there as soon as I can."

"Okay. See you then." Trish disconnected. She'd planned on keeping at least one military man warm. She just hadn't planned on turning him over to Dawn.

This should be interesting.

CHAPTER FOUR

"I told you she was hot." Zippy's eyes were glued to Dawn, or rather Dawn's tits, even as he spoke to Crash.

"And I told you I didn't want to be fixed up."

"Fine. Maybe I'll go for it myself. I'd forgotten how smoking she was."

Crash shook his head. Zippy *going for it* with his sister's best friend sounded like a recipe for disaster to him. If it ended up being a one-night stand, Zip wouldn't be able to help but keep running into the girl because of her friendship with his sister. Same thing if it turned into a longer relationship and ended badly. There'd be hard feelings and no avoiding her. Trish wouldn't like being put in the middle of a messy situation between her best friend and her brother. That was the very reason Crash shouldn't be having the thoughts he had about

Zippy's sister.

Crash had never thought of Zippy as a good-looking guy. He just wasn't wired to think about a fellow Marine like that. But Trish had the same dark hair and rich green eyes her brother had, and on her it was a drop dead gorgeous combination. Add to the knockout hair and eyes Trish's long legs and tits that weren't huge but a perfect mouthful and she was his perfect type.

The damn women had outfitted her killer body to perfection too. The sundress was low enough in front to hint at some cleavage and short enough to be tasteful but still show off a tempting amount of leg.

More than looks, though, she was funny and cute and—shit, she also happened to be his best buddy's sister. Crash had to keep reminding himself of that.

Maybe it was for the best she was off limits. Crash didn't want to be tethered to a relationship back in the States while he was in Afghanistan. That too was a recipe for disaster. Separations like that were hard on an established relationship. Forget about a brand new one just getting off the ground. His last girlfriend had cheated on him while he was stateside—in the same damn town. How could he trust a woman thousands of miles away?

And her being Zippy's sister made one night of fun with her here in the city impossible. Guys didn't do that to each other. If the situations were reversed and Zippy screwed around with Crash's sister and then left for deployment without ever talking to her again, he'd knock Zippy out cold.

Pity, though. He was really enjoying Trish's

company. Watching the way she put Zip in his place was the most fun Crash had had in a while. Half the time Zippy didn't even realize she was manipulating him into doing what she wanted. Yup, Trish was a smart girl wrapped up in one hell of a tempting package.

Crap. He had to stop thinking that kind of shit.

"Who's up for shots?"

"Shots?" Crash's brows drew into a frown at Zippy's question.

Dawn thrust one hand into the air. "I'm in. I'm not driving anywhere tonight."

Zippy glanced from Trish to Crash. "How about you two?"

Trish shook her head. "I don't think so."

"Me either. Thanks."

"Looks like it's just you and me, Dawn." Zippy grinned.

"That's fine with me." Dawn stood and glanced back at the table. "Party poopers."

She flounced off and Trish laughed. "These party poopers won't be the ones with a hangover in the morning."

Crash laughed at the truth of that. "You ain't hardly kidding. That zero-seven-hundred muster is going to come way too early."

"Zero-seven-hundred." Her lips twitched with a smile. "It's funny hearing you say that. Danny doesn't use Marine-speak at home."

"No?" He cringed. "Sorry. I didn't even think about it."

"Don't apologize. It's adorable. I like hearing it." Trish beamed at him.

Well, all righty then. He'd have to sprinkle a few more Marine-isms into his speech if it had her smiling like that and had her thinking he was adorable.

Trish continued, "Anyway, seven on a Saturday morning after they gave you all of Friday night out in the city is pretty unfair."

He laughed. "The military doesn't really recognize weekends. Or what's fair."

She let out a *humph*, looking indignant on his behalf. It was so cute he had to smile…and wish one more time she were anyone besides who she was.

Zippy and Dawn-with-the-double-Ds returned a few minutes later carrying two shots each.

Trish eyed the four glasses. "I thought you weren't getting us shots."

"I didn't. Dawn and I did ours at the bar, then a guy saw my uniform and insisted on buying us a round for the whole table." Zippy cocked a head toward the bar.

"It really would have been rude to say no." Dawn put the two glasses in her hands down and turned to give a little wave to a guy perched on a barstool. He raised his glass in a toast to her and Crash had to wonder if the motivation to buy a round had been Zippy's uniform, or Dawn's cleavage-baring top. Perhaps both. Either way, there now were shots on the table, one in front of each of them.

"What's in these?" Crash stared at the purple liquid in the glass. Purple was not his preferred color when it came to alcohol.

"Who knows?" Zippy shrugged. "It's the special

shot of the night."

It certainly looked special, all right. And frightening. Crash wasn't much for anything other than beer, but when he did do a shot, he could usually see through it. Tequila. Vodka. Something not so colorful.

"What should we drink to?" Dawn grabbed her glass, looking undisturbed by the drink's hue.

Trish picked up hers too and held it, poised in the air. It looked like they were doing this so Crash picked up his glass as she said, "To our brave men and women in uniform. May they all come home safely."

Could she be any more perfect? Crash would drink to that...even the mysterious purple shot. Joining the others, he raised his glass and knocked back the sticky sweet alcohol.

Even though the liquid had been chilled, it still burned a path to his belly. The damn thing might look like a girly drink, but it had a kick to it. That hot dog he'd had hours ago on the walk to the bar had long ago vacated his stomach. Now, he was starting to feel the effects of too many beers and one crazy shot.

He glanced at Trish as she screwed up her face like child who didn't like her medicine. "That thing was horrid. It tastes like..."

When she couldn't come up with the word, Crash said, "Cough medicine?"

"Yes. Exactly. Grape cough medicine from when I was a kid. Ugh. Who thought that was a good idea for a drink?"

Obviously the bartender who'd chosen it for

today's special. Dawn too, now that he took a look at her. She was holding her empty shot glass over her tongue to catch the last drops. Meanwhile, Zippy watched with slack-mouthed intensity.

Crash glanced at Trish. "Looks like your friend has a taste for cough syrup."

"Looks like." Her gaze moved to Zippy. "Looks like my brother has a taste for something too— namely, my friend."

The laugh burst out of Crash before he could control it. Shaking his head, he smiled. He loved a woman who didn't pull any punches. Trish called things like she saw them, and that was all right with him.

"You're right about that." Crash turned away from watching Zippy watch Dawn and toward Trish. "You want something else to drink? I'll get it for you, and I promise when I come back with it, it won't be purple."

"I'll have another beer, if you don't mind getting it."

"A beer it is, my dear." He attempted his best phony Irish accent but it came out tinged with a Southern drawl.

That didn't matter. It still earned him a smile from Trish. Happy for that, he stood and turned to ask the others if they wanted anything. It didn't take long for him to realize there was nothing they wanted that he could provide—Dawn was no longer using her tongue on the shot glass. She was now using it on Zippy.

Crash glanced back at Trish just as, wide-eyed, she shoved her chair back from the table and stood.

"I think I'd better come with you to the bar rather than wait here."

"Yeah." He nodded, not blaming her one bit for that decision. "I think that's a very good idea."

The bar was crowded, and there were a few men looking at Trish with a little too much interest. Crash put a palm on her lower back to guide her across the room and felt her warmth against his hand through the cotton of her shirt.

He was tall, but she wasn't lacking in the height department either. In her shoes, she came up to his chin. Damned if she wouldn't fit him perfect if he wrapped his arms around her and leaned down—

Crap. There he went thinking things he shouldn't again.

Crash couldn't decide if he should drink away this attraction to Trish he felt creeping over him, or stay sober and hope to fight it. Either way the rest of the night in Trish's company while his friend and hers were off sucking face was going to be a challenge, but it sure wouldn't be boring.

~ * ~

"I say we crash in the hotel and go back to the boat in the morning." Over an hour and a few more drinks later Zippy swayed a bit. He, and Dawn beneath the arm he had draped over her shoulder, fell off the curb and into the street.

"I agree." Dawn steered them back onto the sidewalk, but in the process stumbled into a person walking by.

Crash was beginning to think they'd be lucky to get to the hotel, forget about all the way back to where the boat was docked. Theoretically—okay, maybe not so theoretically and more like officially—they were supposed to conduct themselves in a manner above reproach while in uniform.

Somehow, it hadn't worked out that way tonight. By the time they'd left the bar, another guy had bought them a round of beer and another round of shots. Crash hadn't said no to them but he was in far better shape than Zip.

"You'll drive us back to the boat in the morning. Right, sis?"

"Sure." Trish cringed. "What time was that again?"

"We have to be checked in by zero-seven-hundred. We'll have to leave here with enough time to get back."

"That's fine. If we leave a little after six-thirty, we'll make it in plenty of time. There won't be any traffic that early on a Saturday morning. That's for sure."

"You're the best sister ever." There was a definite slur in Zippy words.

"Yeah, yeah." Beneath her breath, just loud enough for Crash to hear, she mumbled, "Getting my brother laid with my best friend—sister of the year, I am."

Crash grinned and realized he should have stopped drinking. That had been a bad decision on his part, because every moment he spent with Trish, the more he liked her.

He reached out and put his hand on the back of her neck. "You are. The coolest sister ever. When Zippy's sober, he'll realize how true that is."

Trish's eyes met his. "Thanks."

Realizing how inappropriate it was to be touching her like this, he let his hand drop. "You gonna be okay with us crashing in your room for the night?"

"It's fine. I chose this hotel because all the rooms are set up like suites with a living area and a little kitchenette. It's nicer than my apartment." Trish eyed her brother and Dawn, who'd gone back to kissing while trying to walk at the same time. They weren't making a very good show of it. "Of course, I'm thinking the walls aren't sound proof."

Obviously Trish didn't want to have to listen to Zippy getting busy with Dawn any more than Crash did. Hopefully, they wouldn't have to. Maybe he could relieve her worry on this front. "You get drunk with your brother a lot?"

"God, no." A frown crinkled the skin between Trish's dark brows.

Crash laughed at her reaction. "Well, I do and I know one thing. He'll go strong until he stops drinking. Then you sit him down someplace comfortable and he crashes hard. Out like a light in a few minutes." Crash tipped a head toward Dawn. "What about her?"

"Not sure. Dawn and I usually have a glass of wine when we go out together, not shots. I guess we can hope she'll fall asleep once he does."

They'd reached the hotel where Trish had parked the car hours ago. He gazed up at the soaring building.

"All right. Sounds like a plan." Crash slapped Zippy on the back to get his attention so he'd stop trying to kiss Dawn while walking into things. Bad enough they were behaving this way in the street. Crash didn't want to make a bad show of it in the lobby too. "Ease up for a second, big guy. We're here. Lead the way, Trish."

After one long elevator ride during which Zippy was all over Dawn, and a short trip down the hall, Trish opened the door and Crash could see she'd been right. The room was damn impressive. Way better than Crash's quarters in the staff barracks back in New River. "Nice."

"Isn't it? So I'm gonna go pull out the sleeper sofa in the living room and set it up for you guys to sleep on."

"Sounds good, sis." Zippy, still semi-attached to Dawn, stumbled through the suite, taking a little self-guided drunken tour. "Wow, look at this place."

Crash shook his head at his friend, then glanced around the space, searching for the door to the bathroom. When he turned back it was to find Trish bent over the couch, her beautiful ass poked temptingly in the air as she divested the sofa of its cushions. Trish sure had curves where they mattered.

He dragged his eyes off her butt. "Um, I'm just gonna hit the restroom."

Still bent at the waist, she twisted to look back at him and he got a view down her shirt, all the way to the lace of her bra. *Christ.* He yanked his gaze away as she said, "Bathroom is through the bedroom."

"Thanks." Blowing out a breath, Crash headed for the bathroom. Hopefully she'd be done with the bending by the time he got back.

Fucking Zippy. It just figured he'd have a hot as hell sister. Damn Crash's luck.

CHAPTER FIVE

Trish tossed the two extra bed pillows she'd found in the closet onto the sofabed and took a step back to admire her work. It didn't look too bad. Yeah, the mattress was thin and with two big men sleeping on it they'd feel every spring, but it would have to do. They'd have a nice air-conditioned place to sleep, sheets, a blanket and pillows. It had to be better than some of the places they'd slept since being in the Marine Corps, so she wasn't going to feel guilty about the quality of the mattress.

"We, uh, have a problem." Crash's voice coming from behind her brought Trish's attention around.

She spun to face him. Was he talking about his makeshift bed for tonight? Maybe he had a bad back and was afraid sleeping on it would mess him up. "What's wrong?"

He hooked a thumb in the direction of the closed

bedroom door and pressed his lips together. "I hate to have to tell you this since he's your brother and all, but Zippy's getting busy with Dawn in your bed."

Her brows rose. "How busy?" Maybe she didn't want to know.

"Let me put it this way, when I came out of the bathroom she had no shirt on and his uniform was in a pile on the floor. It about killed me to not pick it up and hang it, but she was about to—" Crash shook his head and let out a laugh. "Never mind. In any case, I wasn't fixin' to stick around for it."

"All righty." Noise from the bedroom halted whatever more Trish had been about to say. Dawn had a loud voice on a normal day. Drunk, and in the throes of passion, she was even louder.

Crash hiked up one brow and reached for the remote control. "Maybe I should turn on the television."

"Yeah. Good idea. Loud." Trish sat on the edge of the mattress. Maybe Danny had done her a favor. What a perfect excuse to spend more time with Crash.

He grinned and then shook his head. "I really am sorry about this. I know it must not be funny for you."

"It's not your fault. It's my brother and my friend." She drew in a big breath. "So, I guess I'm out here with you for the night."

"You can take the open-up couch. I'll sleep in the chair."

Was that offer from Crash his way of being a gentleman? Or was he simply not interested in sharing the bed with her?

"No, don't be silly. We can both fit on the—" Another sound, this time Danny's voice, filtered through the closed bedroom door.

Crash pushed the remote and raised the volume a little higher. He tossed the control onto the table before turning back to her, looking pained. "Trish, I'm gonna be perfectly honest here. Since I'd planned on sleeping on the boat tonight, I don't have any other clothes with me. I can't sleep in this uniform and still be presentable enough to be seen in it tomorrow morning when I check back in. I'm gonna have to sleep in my underwear."

"I understand that. There's sheets and blankets, if you're worried about modesty."

"That's not the problem." He let out a breath. "I've got enough booze in me that I don't think I can lie next to you without it getting to me. Especially if I have to hear them doing that in there."

A smile twitched her lips at his confession. Nothing like a man admitting he was going to get a hard-on just from being next to you in a bed. Sick as it seemed, Trish was going to take that as compliment. It was more than she'd gotten lately in her woefully pitiful social life. There was a serious man drought in New Jersey. Or maybe Trish was a walking guy repellant. Either way, she'd been sans boyfriend and in fact lacking in any sort of male companionship for far too long.

The man before her looked yummy in his uniform and, she was sure, without it. He was just the recipe to end her fast. She certainly could make a feast out of Crash. "Can I be honest with you too?"

He dipped his head in a nod. "A'ight."

"I understand what you said earlier about not wanting to get involved with anyone right before you deploy and I think you're right about that. But I also believe that two mature, consenting adults can engage in pleasurable activities together without getting involved and it doesn't have to be complicated if they both agree to that condition up front." Trish was fairly impressed with herself.

That had been quite a speech she'd come up with on the fly while her heart was pounding so hard it was beginning to shake her whole body. She watched for a reaction from Crash, and boy did she get it. His mouth dropped open before he clamped it shut again.

His sandy-colored brows drew low. "Um, Trish."

Crap. That was not a promising start to his statement. And he was frowning. She must have misinterpreted everything he'd been trying to say to her before. He wasn't interested. She could tell that by his hesitation now, which meant she'd just made a huge ass of herself and probably made him think she was some sort of loose woman who routinely slept with a guy the first night she met him. A New Jersey 'ho like all the girls on that reality show she hated with a passion. The sad thing was if that were true her sex life wouldn't have been on a year long dry spell.

Trish held up one hand to stop him before he tried to let her down gently. "No, it's fine. I was kidding anyway. A joke that was in bad taste. I guess a few beers and a purple shot and my good sense disappears."

He reached out and wrapped that incredibly big and strong hand around her arm. God, how she'd love to feel those hands all over her body.

"Trish, stop. There's nothing I'd like more than to spend tonight with you, engaging in all sorts of *pleasurable activity*. Believe me. But you're Zippy's sister. That's pretty much the worst thing one guy can do to another guy."

He'd leaned closer while he'd spoken, keeping his voice low and just for her, as if Danny could have heard them anyway over the sound of the television and Dawn's moaning.

His hand remained on her arm. Warm. Strong. It had her insides heating. She found herself leaning closer to him. "First of all, I'm my own person and I make my own decisions. Second, what Danny doesn't know won't hurt him."

Crash swallowed. His gaze dropped to her lips before he pulled it back up. His eyes were narrowed as they captured and held hers. "I guess all it takes is a few beers and some purple shots to do in my good sense too."

As he moved closer, Trish's pulse vibrated her from within. This was going to happen and damn, she couldn't think of anything she wanted more.

His eyes remained on her until their mouths touched with the spark of barely held restraint on both their parts. She'd imagined but hadn't allowed herself to assume this would happen, but now his hand was in her hair and he was angling his mouth across hers.

His tongue slipped between her lips and the kiss

rocketed to another level. She couldn't help the moan that escaped her. The sound had him pulling back and drawing in a shuddering breath.

Crash cradled the back of her head with his palm as, breathing hard, he leaned his forehead against hers. "You sure you want this?"

"Yes. You?"

"Oh, God, yes."

He leaned back and started to unbutton his short-sleeved khaki shirt. She watched as each button opened revealed more of the tight, white T-shirt stretched across the muscles of Crash's hard body beneath.

It was like a ritual watching him undress. The uniform shirt came off but it didn't go on the floor like Danny's had. Crash hung his on the back of the desk chair. He even adjusted the shoulders so it hung straight. The belt and pants came off next. Those got draped just as neatly over the back of another chair. His black shoes, still looking shiny and polished even though they'd been walking around in the dirty city all day, he lined up beneath the desk. He'd taken off his cover the moment they'd entered the building. That sat on the desk where he'd laid it when they first walked in.

Crash glanced up and caught her watching. He cocked a brow as his gaze dropped to take her in from head to toe. She realized she'd yet to take anything off herself. That could come later. She was enjoying the show now. Besides, maybe he'd like to help her get undressed. That might be nice.

His black socks came off. He laid those over his shoes and then took off his wristwatch. That left him in nothing but his underwear and a T-shirt when he walked toward her, closing the distance in a few long strides. Her breath came in short bursts as he put his hands on her waist, leaned down and took her mouth.

Those hands didn't stay idol as he kissed her. He gathered up the fabric of her dress and raised it over her hips, all the way to her waist. She felt the cool air of the room brush the skin, newly exposed as he pushed higher. He leaned away from the kiss and pulled her sundress up and over her head.

He shook it out and carried the dress to the far arm of the sofa where he draped it carefully. Trish's lips twitched with amusement. She understood the care he'd taken with his uniform—he had to put it back on in the morning and he needed to look presentable when he checked in. But for him to take such care with her dress gave her the impression this wasn't about the uniform. This was Crash. This was the real him. Obsessively neat and absolutely adorable.

The smile finally won out and spread across her face so wide there was no hiding it so she figured she'd better say something. "Are you going to fold my bra and underwear too?"

Those sandy brows rose until his lips curved in a smile. "Maybe. Let's take them off and find out."

He came back to stand toe to toe with her, so close they almost touched. So close he had to lean away to pull his T-shirt over his head. She waited and watched the conflict visible in his expression as he held the shirt.

"Go on. You can hang it over the chair. I know it

will kill you if you don't and I want all of your attention on me, not on thinking if your shirt will be wrinkled in the morning."

"Thank you." Crash spun to the desk chair, shaking out the shirt with one brisk flip of his wrists as he walked. While he went, she got a look at the tattoos the shirt had hidden. An eagle, globe and anchor on his back. A confederate flag on one shoulder. An American flag on the other shoulder. She liked them. She'd have to take a closer look. Later, when she wasn't so distracted by other things, such as anticipating what this bad boy could do to her with that tattooed body of his.

The T-shirt neatly draped over the chair and safe from wrinkles, he was back to her in an instant, gloriously shirtless with all those tempting, hard muscles exposed. She ran her hand up the skin of his chest, moving her fingers over the fine blond hair covering him.

He reached around and unhooked her bra before sliding it down her arms and clear of her fingertips. Holding it out to the side, he dangled the item from one finger. Wearing a smirk, he let it drop to the ground.

She smiled. "Very good. I'm impressed."

"You ain't seen nothing yet." Crash lifted her as if she weighed nothing, tossing her onto the mattress and following her down.

As his body covered hers, she spared a brief thought that they shouldn't be rolling around mostly naked right out in the open in the living area. Her brother was in the next room. But so was Dawn, and the bathroom was in the bedroom, so why would

Danny come out here? She couldn't think of a single good reason he or Dawn would leave the bedroom and discover her and Crash.

That was good because the last thing she wanted was for this to be interrupted. Trish forgot her worries about her brother as Crash's weight pressed her into the mattress. He slid one of his legs between her thighs, parting them.

God, it had been too long since she'd had a man over her or between her legs. And it was very possible she'd never had a man quite as manly as Crash ever. Idiosyncrasies aside, he oozed masculinity. She felt it in his every touch. In his kiss as his lips possessed hers, soft at first, and then harder, more demanding.

In between punishing kisses and thrusts of his tongue against hers, he pulled back far enough to say, "I leave in a couple of weeks."

"I know. It's okay."

His blue eyes focused on hers. "Predeployment sex can get pretty wild."

If that was meant to be a warning to get her to change her mind, it did the opposite. He'd only made Trish want it more. "That's fine. Go for it."

Crash groaned. "Oh, God, you're perfect."

He moved down her body and closed his mouth over one of her breasts. She hissed in a breath when he tugged her nipple with his teeth. Sex with a man about to leave for a seven-month deployment that held no possibilities for sex of any kind . . . Just the thought had her getting wet.

He moved lower, down her stomach, his mouth spreading heat over every inch of skin it touched.

She grasped for his head and felt the soft brush of his cropped hair against her palms. He slid his hands down her torso to hook his fingers beneath the waistband of her underwear. She knew any second that last item of clothing was going to end up on the floor next to her bra. With any luck, his boxer briefs would join them there shortly.

Crash paused with his hands so temptingly close to baring her to him. "I need you to know something."

"Okay." Trish could think of far better uses for Crash's mouth than talking, but he had something to say, so she was willing to listen. Besides, he could talk all he wanted, as long as he finished taking her underwear off some time in the near future.

"I have a couple of condoms in my pocket, but that's because Zip—uh, the guys—made me bring them. Medical gives tons of them out for free on the boat whenever we pull into a port."

Trish smiled. He was so cute, not wanting to tell her it was Danny who'd been the guy who gave him condoms.

"All right."

"I just wanted you to know that I didn't come packing—with the condoms, I mean—because I was expecting something like this to happen. I wasn't."

"Thank you for telling me."

Thanks to Danny too, as weird as that felt. Now, Trish wouldn't have to worry about protection. She could enjoy Crash without fear of consequences. They had what they needed because of her brother's quest to get himself and his friend some action on their trip to the Big Apple.

It would have been nice to think Danny had been most excited about seeing his dear sister before deploying, not about getting laid on this trip, but she'd get over it. Being with Crash would definitely help her move past that slight.

"Anything else you need to confess?" she asked.

A self-deprecating smile on his lips, Crash dropped his chin. When he raised his gaze to hers again, he said, "No. I'm done."

"Not quite, you're not." She glanced pointedly at her underwear.

He let out a short laugh. "I'm done talking. I haven't even begun with the rest."

Trish smiled. "That's very good to hear."

Crash pulled her underwear down and there was no more smiling because things were beginning to get serious. Trish ached from wanting to be filled by him and as if he could sense that, he slid his fingers into her.

His eyes narrowed. He hissed in a breath through his teeth as he stroked in and out of her. "I need to be inside you."

"That can be arranged." She licked her lips, her mouth dry just from thinking about it.

His gaze focused on the action. With a groan he moved back up her body and crashed his mouth against hers. Reaching between them, he zeroed in on her clit, working her with his fingers even as his mouth worked hers. His fingers were large, but they handled the delicate task beautifully.

His touch was light to start, waking up her tight little bundle of nerves slowly, circling her first in one direction, and then the other. As the pressure of his fingers on her increased, so did her pleasure. His touch sped faster and her muscles bore down, coiling for release. She tipped her hips. He took the cue and responded by working her harder.

Her breath began to come in quick bursts as he brought her closer to orgasm. She was gasping for breath and bucking against him when he broke the kiss. He latched his teeth onto his lower lip and intensified the speed of his fingers as he studied her face. He was going to watch her as she came and there was nothing she could do about it. Trish couldn't think about that much more as she felt her muscles clench and the climax broke free, sending her body into incredible spasms of pure ecstasy.

"Shh." Crash shushed her before his mouth covered hers again and she realized she'd been making much too much noise considering her brother was just a wall away.

Crash didn't let up on her though. He kept working her, pushing her to the next level of pleasure, all while he muffled her cries with his kiss.

She was weak and breathless when he finally eased his touch on her over-sensitized body, but he didn't go far. He slid two fingers inside her and groaned. "So wet."

He wasn't kidding. Trish could feel the truth of his statement. She echoed his groan, waiting for what he'd promised her before he'd taken the detour to make her come—him inside her. "Maybe you should take advantage of that."

"I'm not going to last. I know that already."

"Then we'll have to do it again. You said you have two condoms?"

"Yeah, I got two." His voice sounded gruff, husky with need.

"Good." And good thing Danny was very thorough in his equipping them for this trip. "Put one on."

For a big man, Crash moved fast. He was up and across the room in no time, pulling the foil packets out of his pants. He shoved his boxer briefs down his legs, stepped out of them and left them on the floor where they'd landed.

Yes, there was at least one thing more important to Crash than neatness. Trish was happy to see sex rated higher on his list than properly putting away his underwear. There was something else she was happy to see as well. He was hard and ready for action.

He tossed one packet onto the table next to them and tore into the other. She watched him roll it down his length. Maybe she'd offer to put in on him for the next round. There would definitely be a second time if she had anything to say about it, and if Danny and Dawn stayed put.

A renewed sense of urgency hit. She wanted him in her now before anything happened to interrupt this. Crash didn't make her wait. He was covered and ready, and moving over her again. She spread her legs and made space for him between them.

Braced on one arm, he slid the other beneath the small of her back, raising her off the mattress and driving into her with one hard thrust. Her back bowed with the force of it and the relief at finally being filled after lusting after this man for hours. He repeated the move, plunging inside, over and over, driving her beyond reason until she no longer thought, only felt. Until he was grunting out every labored breath he took, before he plunged deep and held there.

She felt the shudder pass through him as he came buried deep inside her. Felt his elbow give out and his weight crush her. But what was most important was that she felt. After endless hour upon hour and day upon day of a life that seemed to consist of not much more than work and home, punctuated by the obligatory weekly phone call to the parents and the equally scheduled girls night out each weekend with Dawn, Trish had done something just for herself.

It went against everything she'd always thought she believed in, but this one night of crazy predeployment sex with a man she'd just met made her feel more alive than she had in years. She didn't want that feeling to end, but they'd already agreed that it would. It had to. He was leaving. Her heart clenched with that thought.

"Sorry." He rolled to one side.

She missed the weight of him immediately. "For what?" she managed to ask.

"I was crushing you." Crash left his hand on her stomach. She covered it with hers and saw how small her own looked on top of his.

"It's fine. I was kind of hoping you'd crush me again later tonight."

He leaned close and hovered near her mouth. "A'ight. I think that can be arranged."

"Mmm, and tomorrow night too?" she asked.

They'd agreed to uncomplicated predeployment sex, not to a one-night stand specifically. She didn't see any reason it couldn't continue through the weekend, and then end. He'd go back to North Carolina with Danny to get ready to deploy, and she'd head back to New Jersey and her boring life.

Crash wrinkled his nose. "Probably not.

The answer was like a direct blow to her chest. "Oh, okay."

His expression grew soft and he brought his hand up to brush the side of her face. "Not because I don't want to. Believe me. I just don't see how we could make it work."

Because they'd agreed not to get serious and apparently in his mind one night was casual, but two was serious.

Trish nodded. "I understand."

Not really, but . . .

Crash let out a sigh. "It sucks but we've got this damn Cinderella liberty tomorrow night so we have to be back on board the boat by midnight."

Trish's spirits rose along with her brows. Crash wanted to be with her, he just couldn't. "Oh. I didn't realize that. I thought you had all night again."

He shook his head. "Nah. We leave the following morning for home. I guess they don't want us out all night getting shitty. Suppose I can't say I blame them. We're taking the bird home. Don't want to be flying with a hangover on no sleep."

"Yeah." His mention of Cinderella had an image of glass slippers and a ball gown spinning through her mind. It was so incongruous with the manly man beside her, she couldn't help but smile.

He noticed. "What?"

"Sorry, I just found the Cinderella part funny."

He grinned. "You mocking my very official USMC terminology, woman?"

"I guess I am."

"Mmm, well I'm no Prince Charming, but I sure hope I showed you a good time at the ball."

"I think you better show me again."

"Hold on tight to your glass slippers, because that's exactly what I'm fixin' to do." His tempting lips curved up in a smile as he leaned low, closing in for a kiss.

Who needed Prince Charming when she had a Marine dedicated to making her happy for the night? If only it wouldn't all end at midnight tomorrow. Trish was feeling more like Cinderella than she'd ever imagined she could.

~ * ~

The bedroom door flung open and Zippy stumbled through. "Holy shit, what time is it? Are we late?"

Crash cocked a brow. "No, because one of us remembered to set the alarm on his phone last night."

Zippy perused him from head to toe. Crash was done dressing except for his shoes and his cover. "And were you going to wake me any time soon? Or wait until the last minute and then laugh at me as I ran around like a chicken without a head?"

"Don't get your panties in a twist. We have plenty of time." Crash grinned. It was extra funny since that's all Zippy was wearing—his panties or rather his tighty whities. "I was fixin' to wake you as soon as Trish got back.

Meanwhile, Crash had already showered this morning before putting his uniform back on. Tiptoeing through the bedroom in the dark to get to the bathroom all while trying not to see the two tangled bodies on the bed had been like a recon mission, but he'd made it in and back without waking them.

He'd set the alarm for zero-five-thirty. More than enough time to get dressed and then to the boat. He'd honestly set it so early in case they were in the mood for a little something this morning. That hadn't worked out. They'd gone through his only two condoms last night. There were plenty of other creative solutions to enjoying each other without the need for protection, but it hadn't felt right in the light of morning with goodbye looming so close ahead.

Zippy frowned. "Where is Trish anyway?"

"There's free coffee downstairs. Trish went to get us four." The gentleman in Crash had him adding, "I offered to go instead, but she insisted I'd never get the sugar-creamer ratio right for hers."

He'd fought her on that but then she pointed out that of the two jobs—getting coffee for the four of them versus waking Zippy after a hard night—she'd have the easier duty. Having woken up Zip quite a few times, Crash had to agree with her, so he'd stayed behind.

"Yeah, probably not. She's a coffee Nazi, that girl. One bad cup of coffee and she's a raving bitch all day long."

Objecting to Zippy using that term in relation to

his sister and the woman Crash had spent the night with, he responded to it with nothing more than a grunt, before he asked, "Dawn still sleeping?"

"Yeah, which is better actually. We can go back to the ship without the big goodbye scene."

Crash's eyes widened. "You're sneaking out without saying goodbye?"

Zippy's brows drew low. "So what? It's not like I won't see her again. She's Trish's best friend."

"Exactly, dickhead."

Which is why Zippy shouldn't have touched that girl with a ten-foot pole, forget about with his dick. Then again, Trish was just as off limits given who she was. Still, the difference remained that Crash wasn't going to sneak out on her. And they'd gone into last night agreeing it was just a casual thing. No expectations on either of their parts. He wasn't sure Zippy could say the same thing about Dawn.

"I'll apologize next time I'm home in Jersey."

"After we get back from deployment next January?" Then a thought struck Crash. "Wait, aren't we meeting Trish and Dawn again this afternoon after they cut us loose from the boat?"

"I hope not. I wanted to hit up that girlie club I saw the billboard for across the street from where the boat is docked. I think Trish only got the room for the one night anyway."

He couldn't exactly tell Zippy that during his time in bed last night, in between their two energetic bouts of sex, Trish had asked if they'd be together again tonight, which is why he'd assumed she had the room for another night.

"A'ight, but I thought she was here until

Sunday."

"Whatever. I'll ask her when she gets back." Zippy dismissed the subject with a shrug. "I'm jumping in the shower. I wouldn't mind if you brought that coffee in to me when she gets back."

"Yeah. Okay." Crash let out a snort. Him, deliver coffee to Zippy so he can drink it in the shower? Yeah, right. Over his dead body.

The sound of the key in the door signaled Trish was back and that Zippy could get his own damn coffee.

She pushed the door open, a cardboard tray with four cutouts holding to-go coffee cups in her hand. She spotted her brother and smiled. "Good morning, sunshine. How's your head this fine day?"

"Just give me the coffee." Zippy reached for one.

She pulled the tray away. "Nope. That one's mine. The others are light and sweet. Take one of those. And how about a thank you?"

"Thank you."

She rolled her eyes at him. "You're welcome."

"I'm taking a shower."

"Be my guest. And give this to Dawn on your way."

Zippy made a face at that but took the second cup and disappeared through the bedroom door.

"I swear he's so ungrateful. He has sex with the girl and he doesn't even want to bring her the coffee I went downstairs to get?" Trish shook her head.

"Last report was that Dawn's still sleeping anyway." Crash stood and took the cardboard tray from her hand, setting it down on the television stand. He took the one Trish had said was hers out of the holder and turned to hand it to her. "But I, for one, am very grateful. Thank you for getting this. And I still wish you'd let me go, or at least come with you to help carry."

She took the cup and waved away his concern with one hand. "It was nothing. And you're welcome."

"So, I was talking to Zippy about plans for later today. He wasn't sure if you had the room for another night. You going to be around tonight or did you have to get home?" Crash sipped at the hot coffee and tried to look casual. As if he wasn't hanging all of his hopes on her sticking around today so he could spend more time with her.

Even if they couldn't do anything more than hang out, it was still preferable to Zippy's plan—them going to that strip place that masqueraded as a gentleman's club. No doubt that would cost them a fortune for the night, if not in cover charge then in drink prices. Crash didn't understand the attraction of staring at naked women he couldn't touch. Nope. He'd be just fine sitting at an Irish pub with a cold pint and talking to Trish.

"I do have the room for another night. Dawn and I were planning on making a girls' weekend of it. So yeah, we can hang out with you guys until you have to be back on the ship at midnight, Cinderella." She grinned. "If the wicked witch in there says it's okay with him."

Crash put his cup down on the table and took a step forward, then another, until he was close enough to reach out and brush his thumb across Trish's cheek. "You're mixing your fairy tales, for one. If anything, Zippy would be the evil stepmother in this scenario. But besides that, I don't give a damn what he says about it. I want to hang out with you tonight."

He leaned low and brushed his lips across hers, stifling a groan. Now was not the time to be tempted to get anything started with her. One, they were out of condoms, and two, Zippy had already turned off the water in the shower.

Crash forced himself to drop his hand from her face and moved back to where he'd left his coffee, but not before he saw the look in her eyes. She wanted him as much as he wanted her and that made it suck doubly much that it wasn't going to happen tonight. Christ, maybe not ever. At least not for the next seven months while he was in Afghanistan.

Being with her last night was either the best or the worst decision he'd made in a long time. He'd deploy with some damn good memories, but right now, all he felt was a yearning he wasn't going to be able to satisfy.

Unless . . . The evil thought careened into his brain and made him both gleeful and embarrassed at the same time. It was risky. It was horrible, and dammit he wasn't going to be able to stop himself. He was going to do it.

"Trish."

"Yeah."

"I think I have a plan. Something that might get us some more time alone together tonight."

"Sounds intriguing." A smile bowed her lips. "I'm all ears."

CHAPTER SIX

"Liberty call! Liberty call!" The voice of the Boatswain's mate reverberated throughout the ship's communications system. Most announcements onboard were loud and annoying, but nobody minded hearing liberty call.

"Sixteen-thirty? They couldn't let us go a little earlier? Jesus. It's our last night here. It's bad enough we only have until midnight." Zippy stormed down the narrow passageway on the boat as fast as a man could walk.

"Guess we should be happy it wasn't later." Crash was as anxious to get the hell out of there as Zippy was, he just couldn't show it quite as enthusiastically. Not since the reason Crash wanted off that boat was so he could see Zippy's sister again. Before that happened there were a number of things he needed to do, chief among them procuring more condoms without Zippy seeing. For all Zip knew, Crash should still have the two he'd given him yesterday.

Crash followed Zippy through the confined spaces, heading toward the berthing and their assigned quarters. Even after the day spent on board, he was still very much aware of that same funky smell every military vessel he'd ever been on had. Not that New York City smelled like a rose, but it would be nice to get away from the boat for a while.

They reached their racks and changed from their cammies into Charlies. As the minutes ticked by, Crash knew he was running out of time to do what he needed to do. He should have tried to sneak off to Medical some time during the day and grabbed a strip of condoms for himself, but it seemed Zippy had been up his ass all day.

Crash needed to stall. "I, uh, wanna brush my teeth before we go."

Zippy leveled an unhappy gaze at him. "More than half the day is already gone and you're worried about oral hygiene?"

"We're going out to the club after we have dinner with your sister, right? You can do what you want, but I don't want a lap dance from a woman who looks as hot as the girls on that billboard with a day's worth of stink on my breath." Crash could pull an attitude as well as Zippy could. He cocked a brow. "Do you?"

Zippy blew out a breath. He reached into the small locker and pulled out his shaving bag. "All right. Let's just both be quick about it."

Crash eyed the bag in Zippy's hand. That was where the condoms were. Crap. How was he going to steal any out of there if Zip took it with him? As his brain reeled for a solution Zippy reached in and pulled out his toothbrush and toothpaste. That meant he'd leave the bag there, unattended.

He needed Zippy to leave him alone for just a few seconds. "Well, by all means. Don't let me hold you up. Go. I'll grab my stuff and be right behind you."

"Fine. But hurry up." Another scowl and Zippy was off toward the head.

Zippy was barely clear from view when Crash grabbed the bag off the middle one of the three bunks spaced painfully close together. Luckily, a strip of about six attached foil packets were folded neatly inside.

Crash had just torn off two and was trying to decide if the strip looked different enough that Zippy would notice when he heard voices coming toward him.

Damn boat. No privacy whatsoever. There was absolutely no place a man could go that there wasn't already someone else there, or on his way there.

With no more time to worry, Crash shoved the strip back inside the bag and tossed it on the rack where Zippy had left it just as two Marines came down the passageway. For once the passages being narrow and hard to walk through had worked in Crash's favor. It had given him enough time to not get caught doing something he shouldn't be doing.

He nodded to the two men as they stopped. "Y'all heading ashore?"

The two Marines stared at Crash like he had dick antlers. One answered, "Yeah. Aren't you?"

"Yup." Admittedly, it was a stupid question. Who in his right mind would stay on the boat when they had liberty in New York City? Crash tried to recover from looking like an idiot. He remembered his original ruse to get rid of Zippy. He reached into his own locker and pulled out the small black bag he'd stashed there. "Just gonna brush these chicklets of mine and then head out."

The Marines had moved on to their own business. While one stood by waiting, the other one unlocked the lid beneath the mattress platform in the bottom coffin rack. Lifting the lid, he reached inside and pulled out his wallet. He realized Crash was still standing there like a fool and shot him a glance. "All right. We'll see you later."

"Right. Later." With the condoms still hidden in his fist and his shaving bag held in the crook of one arm like a running back held a football, Crash left the two. He strode down the passageway, his rubber-soled shoes moving over the non-skid floors as fast as he could go.

As Crash stashed the condoms in his pocket he realized he'd gotten away with it. Or at least with part one of his plan. There was much more to do to make tonight turn out the way he hoped it would. Yeah, he felt guilty. In the span of twenty-four hours he'd lied, stolen, and slept with his best friend's sister. The worst part was, he couldn't wait to see Trish again. More than just see her. Crash couldn't wait to commit that last sin at least one more time. Maybe two.

Not his fault, really. She was a smart, sexy, funny woman. A girl who was great to hang out with, who also happened to be nice to look at. Then there was the unbelievable sex they'd had that he couldn't wait to have again. He blamed that part— how he ached to sink himself deep inside her so badly it nearly hurt—on the impending deployment. He'd just have to move on from the guilt over that. Time to get this night started.

Crash deflected Zippy's annoyance at his taking too long and managed to actually get his teeth brushed. He ignored his friend and took the extra time to gargle with mouthwash too. He planned on doing some kissing tonight, and he didn't want Trish's last memory of him before he left to be bad breath.

Okay, maybe he was worrying about the wrong things. He should be more concerned about his plan not working. Getting Zippy and Dawn drunk enough they'd fall back into bed together so Crash could grab some alone time with Trish was bad enough. But then he'd have to somehow get Zippy back on board in that condition without either of them getting into trouble and possibly losing Crash his best friend.

Zippy was standing in the passageway by their racks when Crash got back from brushing his teeth. "Come on. Hurry up. I wanna get this dinner with my sister over with so we can say our goodbyes and get to the club."

"Calm the hell down. I'm done." Crash tossed his bag into the locker and grabbed his cover. Turning, he shot Zippy a look as they made their way toward the hanger deck. It couldn't hurt to plant the seed of an idea in Zippy's horny brain. "You know, I thought you'd be happy to get another shot with Dawn tonight. Why are you so eager to ditch her?"

"This is the city that never sleeps. Who wants to be tied down on our last night here?"

Crash did. He'd be very happy to spend his last night here with Trish, rather than going to some overpriced strip club where he could look and not touch. He wouldn't even mind if Trish tied him down—literally. Hell, he was open-minded. He wasn't opposed to trying something once.

"Whatever you say. You tell your sister we've been cut loose?"

"Yeah. She texted that she's here already."

Hearing that had Crash's heart rate and his pace speeding up. He shot Zippy a sideways glance and hoped the anticipation of seeing Trish again wasn't showing all over his face.

When had he totally lost his cool around women? He should be able to see her again without getting as breathless as a schoolgirl. Then again, the memory of being with her last night was so fresh that if he concentrated hard enough, he could bring to mind all the vivid details. The sound of her coming, the heat of her surrounding him, the softness of her skin and the passion of her mouth beneath his.

Crap. Now he was getting hard. Crash drew in a breath and gave himself a mental slap. They still needed to check out, and with them all getting cut loose at the same time it was taking a while to get off the boat.

He and Zippy joined the masses on the hanger deck inching along in the line that had no doubt begun to form at the sound of liberty call nearly twenty minutes ago. The men waiting engaged in small talk as they crept forward, ramping downward to the level below where the Officer of the Day stood his watch on the quarterdeck.

Finally, Crash and Zippy reached the OOD. Crash stood at attention in front of the duty, held his ID up with his left hand and snapped into a well-practiced salute with his right. "Permission to go ashore, sir."

The OOD returned the salute. "Permission granted."

Crash executed a facing movement and stepped from the quarterdeck to the top of the brow. Making a sharp turn to the front of the ship, he saluted the flag, faced back down the gangplank and stepped off. Zippy, having repeated every one of Crash's steps was close behind.

Then they were free, striding down the brow that shook with the steps of so many Marines and Sailors eager to get to their goal—the pleasures of New York. Crash didn't have to go very far to find his objective. When they reached the curb he spotted the now familiar car with the New Jersey license plates. Trish stood beside it, looking amazing in another dress. This one pink and a little lower cut in the front. Short enough that, with the high heels, her legs looked a mile long.

When he could pull his gaze away from Trish, he noticed Dawn and tried not to let his reaction to her outfit show on his face. Trish must have been working a plan of her own, one that complimented his perfectly. Dawn was dressed to impress. Or at least to attract a man with a breast fetish like Zippy. Crash knew instinctively, even before seeing her satisfied grin, that Trish had a hand in how Dawn looked today.

He grinned, and when they were closer, his smile only got wider when he saw the devilish expression cross her face.

"Hi. About time they let you two go." Trish accepted her brother's hug.

"Yeah, I know. Tell me about it," Zippy grumbled.

When Zippy stepped back, she turned to Crash. She wrapped her arms around his waist as he stiffened. He glanced at Zippy and saw he'd moved on to saying hello to Dawn. With the amount of cleavage she was sporting, Crash figured he had a few seconds leeway with Trish.

"Hey." She smiled up at him and he was happy for the two condoms in his pocket, because if presented with the opportunity there was no way he'd give up the opportunity to be with this woman.

"Hey." Crash squeezed her tight, enjoying the feel of her in his arms before he forced himself to let her go and take a step back. He realized he was being rude and yanked his focus off Trish long enough to be polite to her friend. "Hey, Dawn."

"Crash. Nice to see you again."

Since she'd slept through his departure this morning, he supposed she could have been embarrassed that the last time he'd seen her she'd been stumbling drunk and attached at the lips to his buddy. But one look at her confidant strut as she walked in her mile-high heels around the car, swaying in the hips the entire way, told him she definitely was not that type to get embarrassed, which was fine. More power to her and even better for his plan for a repeat of last night.

"I made a reservation at the Irish pub next to my hotel. They've got killer shepherd's pie, and drink specials and live music tonight." Trish glanced at Crash. "Dollar shots before six."

He stopped, one hand on the door handle of the car. "Purple ones?"

"I sure hope so." Trish shot him a grin and then got into the driver's seat.

Crash couldn't help the smile that got so big his face was going to start to hurt soon if he didn't control it. She wanted the time with him as much as he wanted the time alone with her, and she'd done her research. Dollar shots right next door to the hotel—plans for tonight were sure looking good.

~ * ~

Trish leaned toward Crash in the red vinyl booth and angled her mouth toward his ear. "They're getting drunk."

"Yes, they are." Truth be told, so was Crash. Not exactly drunk, but definitely feeling the effects.

He could get away with nursing one beer, but when the rounds of shots kept coming, it would have seemed suspicious if Crash had refused to partake while he kept pushing them on Zippy.

Still, things were going just as planned. Having the shots before the food arrived only helped his case with Zippy and Dawn. The two were on the dance floor grinding against each other. Only a matter of time now. Crash glanced at his watch. Nearly nineteen-hundred hours.

"What time is it?" Trish hadn't missed the move. They were both more than conscious of their limited time tonight.

"Almost seven o'clock," Crash answered.

"I don't like this Cinderella liberty." Her pout drew his gaze to her lips.

"Me either."

Trish let out a deep sigh. "Even if Dawn can keep Danny distracted so he doesn't want to leave early to go to that club you told me about, we should still leave no later than eleven-thirty to make sure you're not late. Just in case we hit traffic."

"Yeah." He didn't want to talk about leaving. He also didn't want to be here in public where he couldn't touch her the way he wanted.

Then again, the bar was dim, lit by a few hanging lamps and some neon signs. Crash moved his hand to her thigh, hidden by the table in front of them. A sly smile curved her lips as she rested her hand on his leg, then moved it farther up until just the tip of her finger brushed the crotch of his pants.

His eyes widened before he forced his expression to be neutral. If she wanted to play, he could play. He bunched the fabric of her dress and inched it up. His fingertips brushed the warm skin on the inside of her thigh. She drew in a breath and let it out.

In this very public place, while he kept his gaze trained on her brother on the dance floor, Crash pushed higher until he hit the lace of her underwear. She spread her legs just a bit wider and he started to sweat. Hard as a rock now, he was throbbing behind the fabric of his uniform pants while she ran her finger up and down the outline of his length.

Damn, this was a turn on. He had a feeling it was only going to get hotter, because he had no plans of stopping. Crash slipped beneath the edge of her panties. She was hot and wet, and all for him. He slid between her lips. Her hand on him faltered before she resumed her slow, light stroke over the pants hiding his erection. He didn't treat her quite so gently. With the tip of one finger he zeroed in on her clit, flicking it fast and hard. She jumped beneath his touch but didn't close her legs or push him away.

"How're ya doing?" He glanced her direction, before forcing himself to keep an eye on Zippy.

"Fine." She swallowed hard enough for him to hear her throat working.

"Good." Crash slid a finger inside her, and then a second. He stroked in and out until he heard her draw in a sharp breath. He went back to her clit, circling the tiny nub fast. It wasn't the ideal angle or position for this, but he managed it.

One quick glance at Trish, biting her lower lip, told him it was working. He reversed direction, circling the other way, and felt her jump. She angled her hips, tipping them just a bit, and he heard the tiniest of moans escape her throat. He moved faster. Harder. She was going to come. Right here, right now. At least she would if he had anything to do with it. But good lord, it might just kill him if she did.

She came apart slowly. It started with tiny

thrusts of her hips and moved to her clenching her thighs, but he didn't let up. He kept at it until she was trembling from the effort to stay silent and control her expression. She wasn't as good at controlling her breathing. He heard every closed-mouthed breath tinged with a tiny sound of pleasure that twisted the need inside him tighter. It was by far the most incredible thing he'd ever experienced with a woman in what had been a long and sordid life.

Finally, he eased up on her. He righted her dress and she sagged against the back of the booth. Her hand had stayed in his lap throughout it all, clenched in a tiny fist as she'd come. Now, she spread her fingers over him again and stroked his length. Her touch on him grew firmer and quickened.

Her effort had him smiling. "Trying to get back at me?"

"Mmm, hmm." She shot him a sideways glance.

"Not gonna work, darlin'." Not that he minded her trying. He grinned. "These pants are too thick."

"You won't have pants on later." She pulled her finger away and raised the beer bottle to her lips with one shaky hand.

No, he certainly hoped he wouldn't have pants on later. Crash wanted to guarantee that. In fact, the sooner the better. He raised one hand to signal the waitress.

Trish frowned. "What are you doing?"

"Knocking your brother out for the count." Crash knew exactly how to do that. Enough with the waiting. It was time to get serious.

Trish's brows rose. "Okay."

The waitress arrived. "Yes, sir?"

"A double tequila on the rocks." He glanced at Trish and tipped his head toward Dawn on the dance floor. "What's her downfall?"

"Cosmopolitans."

He glanced back at the waitress. "And one of those, please. Got that?"

"Yes, sir. I'll be right back with your drinks."

"Thanks." As she left for the bar, Crash eyed the dance floor one more time. The two unknowing victims of their plan only had eyes for each other.

Perfect.

CHAPTER SEVEN

Danny's eyelids drooped as the level of tequila in the glass moved lower and the minutes ticked by.

Trish was keenly aware of the time passing, every second bringing them closer to midnight. She had no intention of letting Crash go without at least an hour alone with him. Three hours would be even better. Hating the deadline hanging over their heads, she felt the pressure and searched for some way to get her brother moving.

"Hey, you guys want to run upstairs to the hotel room with me? These shoes are killing me. I want to change them real quick."

"Sure. We'll come with you." Obviously wise to her motivation, Crash stood.

Danny, still seated with his arm around Dawn at the table, frowned. "Can't you go do that and come back here?"

"I think we should go with her. Um, my feet hurt too." Dawn caught Trish's gaze and mouthed silently, "Thank you."

Dawn must have thought Trish was trying to arrange it so she and Danny could have time together in the room. That worked for Trish. As long as the result was time with Crash alone and at least partially naked, it was fine with her.

"Okay. Fine." Danny stood and swayed a bit, his eyes not quite focused. "Did we pay the bill?"

"Yeah. We're all set." Trish cringed and glanced at Crash. Maybe they'd done too good of a job getting her brother liquored up. How was he going to walk back on the ship in this condition?

Crash leaned low. "We got a few hours. He'll be a'ight."

She hoped so. But right now she couldn't worry about how quickly Danny would metabolize the tequila. Trish was more concerned if Dawn could lure him into the bedroom and close the deal so she could be with Crash.

"Come on. Let's go." Trish led the way out of the crowded pub and out onto the sidewalk.

A few steps had them inside the hotel lobby and to the elevators as her heart pounded. Upstairs in the hall outside her room, the adrenaline coursing through her veins had her hand trembling. Trish had to work to hold steady and shove the keycard into the slot in her door. Finally, the light turned green and she turned the knob, pushing the door wide.

Now what? How did she get Danny and Dawn into the bedroom without looking obvious? They were into each other, but unlike last night, they hadn't been making out in the bar, or in the street, or in the elevator . . .

"Danny, can you help me? My other shoes are on the shelf in the closet and I won't be able to reach them." Dawn the seductress batted her eyelashes at Danny.

Trish should have known she wouldn't have to worry about helping her friend get a man into bed. Trish tried not to think too hard about the fact that man was her brother.

"Uh, sure." He glanced back at Crash before Dawn pulled him into the bedroom and closed the door behind them.

Trish shook her head. "Wow, she's good."

"Nuh, uh. You're good. Absolutely amazing." Crash had his hands on her in an instant. "And, oh my God, I thought it would about kill me when you came in the bar."

"You?" She raised a brow. "How do you think I felt? I had to pretend nothing was going on."

Crash dipped lower, his lips just inches from hers. "Oh, there was definitely something going on."

Yes, there was, and she hoped it would happen again. Trish closed the distance and pressed her mouth against his. Crash thrust his tongue between her lips as he backed her up the few feet until she was pressed against the door.

When he broke from her mouth and moved on to biting her neck, she hardly had enough breath to ask, "Should I open the sofabed?"

"No. This is good." He slid down her body until he was on his knees in front of her, his hands moving beneath her dress and up the bare skin of her thighs.

"Don't you want to take off your uniform?" Trish wondered where the fastidious Marine who hung up his T-shirts had gone.

"Too risky. Don't know how long they'll be." Crash pressed his lips against first one thigh, and then the other while his fingers slid over her ass.

"Aren't you worried about messing it up?" It was amazing she could still think given what he was doing to her, but Trish managed it. Barely.

"Doesn't matter. Only have to check in tonight. Tomorrow we'll be in flight suits, and then we'll be home." He pulled down her underwear and there was no more discussion, because his mouth was busy elsewhere.

Crash spread her with his thumbs and drove his tongue into her sensitive flesh. Trish gasped at the feel of it, but she sure as hell didn't want him to stop. She let him know that by moving her feet another step apart and giving him better access. He answered that cue with a low groan.

As much as she wanted this, she wanted him inside her more. "Crash, we don't know how long we have. Just fuck me."

He pulled back and stared up at her, his sandy brows raised high. "You Jersey girls sure say things plain." Then a smile spread across his face. "I like it."

Crash stood and Trish found herself hoisted up against him and carried around the half wall to the kitchenette area. This was good. At least there they would have a little bit of privacy should Danny come out of the bedroom. Crash set her on top of the counter and reached into his pocket.

She watched him tear into one of the condoms he had stashed in his pants. "I see you came packing."

"You have no idea how hard it was to get these without Zippy seeing me." He shook his head as he unbuckled his belt and unzipped his fly. Pushing his underwear down, Crash rolled the latex over his length. His eyes narrowed as he pulled her hips forward and stepped between her spread thighs. "It was well worth the trouble."

Crash pushed inside her with one thrust. After a night of sitting next to him anticipating this moment, and after that orgasm in the bar and his tongue on her just now, she was more than ready.

Eyes closed, Trish let her head fall back against the cabinet behind her and concentrated on the sensations. The feeling of Crash filling her, stroking into her, hard but slow. Fully dressed, he stood on tiptoe to reach her on the counter.

He seemed to throw his whole body into loving her. As he'd said last night, this was predeployment sex. She was sure he was putting everything he had into this, and she was willing to give all she had to him on their last night together.

Crash gripped her hips with both hands and slammed his mouth into hers. His motion into her sped, his breathing increasing along with his stroke. He stiffened beneath the hands she had braced on his arms. She felt the tremor run through him and knew he was coming.

It was as if he came back to his senses once the initial frenzy was over. His sky blue eyes opened and he watched her face. He stayed inside, pressed deep, making the tiniest of motions into her. Wetting one thumb with his tongue, he reached between them and rubbed her clit, slow and gentle.

Trish's eyes drifted shut and her mouth opened on a breath as he zeroed in on the spot that would bring her so much ecstasy. Her muscles were already clenching, primed for release, when Crash pressed harder, working her faster. He leaned close and pulled her earlobe between his teeth, biting just hard enough to let her know he wanted to devour her as much as she wanted him to.

"Oh, God." He let out a breath and she felt the warmth wash over her. "I can feel you squeezing me."

The sound of his voice, the heat of his mouth against her ear, was all it took. Trish felt the climax start to break over her. Her breath came in quick bursts and she couldn't control the sounds of her pleasure.

He was still inside her as they both tried to recover, when she heard the bathroom door close. Her eyes flew open at the sound.

Danny and Dawn were moving around in the other room. They could come through the door any second. She looked to Crash, but he had already pulled out of her and was crossing the small space to toss the used condom in the trashcan.

Eyes wide, he turned to her. "Your underwear."

"Oh my God. It's still by the door. I'll get it." Still in the heels she'd pretended she'd needed to change, Trish jumped down, holding on to the edge of the counter to keep from twisting an ankle.

While Crash was busy tucking in his shirt and zipping his pants, she ran as fast as she could to the door. She spotted the incriminating item on the floor right where Crash had dropped it. Trish bent down and scooped up the scrap of lace. She wadded the fabric into a ball in her fist just as the bedroom door opened and her brother came out wearing the expression she was familiar with from their childhood. The one that looked too innocent to be real, which he donned when he'd been up to no good. It was obvious he and Dawn had done something in there. The only question was why the hell hadn't they taken their time tonight the way they had last night?

"You ready to drive us back to the boat?" he asked, straightening the shirt not so neatly tucked into his pants.

"Already?" Trish put on her own look of innocence.

"Yeah, it's getting late and we have to check in early tonight. Remember?"

"And you want to go out somewhere else before you do." The thought had the acid backing up into her throat.

Why did Danny's plan bother her so much? The reason moved closer to stand behind her now. Crash. She didn't want him at some strip club surrounded by women who for a twenty dollar bill—or however much a damn lap dance cost— would grind their bodies against his.

"I'm sorry, Trish, but I promised some of the guys we'd meet them for a drink at a club near the boat. It's no big deal. You and I got to have dinner together and hang out, didn't we?"

Trish scowled at her brother's lie, or rather avoidance of the complete truth. Crash had told her about Danny's plan to go to the strip club across the street from where the ship was docked. She noticed Danny never had mentioned *which* club he'd be ditching her and Dawn to go to.

"We have time to get down there, Zip. It's early yet." Crash stepped closer and she felt his hand on the small of her back, where her brother couldn't see his touch.

The intimate gesture made Trish more pissed she'd be saying goodbye to him sooner rather than later, thanks to Danny. "It's not like I'm holding you up. As soon as Dawn is ready, we can go."

Danny glanced down at Trish's feet. "I thought you had to change your shoes. That's why we came up here in the first place."

Crap. She'd forgotten about that ruse.

"I do, but the door to the bedroom seemed to be closed for some reason so I couldn't get to my shoes, now could I?" After adding a good dose of attitude to her tone, she strutted around her brother and headed for the bedroom door.

She smothered the guilt and wadded the panties tighter in her hand. She held them behind the skirt of her dress as she walked so he wouldn't see. Trish shouldn't be laying into her brother about being shut inside the bedroom with Dawn since she and Crash had been behaving just as badly together out here without even the privacy of a door.

Right now, she didn't care if she was right or not. All she could think about was the goodbye ahead.

Dawn was still in the bathroom, which was good. It gave Trish time to step behind the closet door and slip her underwear back on. Only then, after she was no longer commando, did she take the time to look for a different pair of shoes. They'd have to be flats since the other pair of heels she'd packed didn't match this dress. Not that it mattered. All she'd be doing was sitting in the car and driving. Delivering her brother and the man she'd been having sex with just minutes before right into the arms of some naked woman-for-hire.

But before they disappeared into the ironically named *gentlemen's* club she'd have to say goodbye to both of them, and that would be the hardest part.

The door to the bathroom opened and she turned to see Dawn, a little pink cheeked, in the doorway, although Trish couldn't say that she wasn't looking a little flushed herself after her own quickie with Crash.

"You ready to go?" Trish asked.

Dawn's brow wrinkled. "Go where?"

"I have to drive them to the dock. Danny is itching to get back."

"Why? I thought they had a few more hours."

"They do." Not in the mood to enable Danny's half truths considering he was taking Crash away from her earlier than necessary, and to be with naked women no less, Trish decided to tell Dawn the real reason. "There's a strip club across the street from their ship he wants to go to."

Dawn's frown deepened. "No wonder he was in such a rush."

"Yup." Trish sat right on the carpet and pulled

off her heels, tossing them one at a time into the closet. She slipped on her flats and stood. "Ready?"

"Yeah. Let's go." Dawn's expression told Trish she was no happier about Danny's plan, and there was nothing either one of them could do about it.

Her brother and the guy she was crushing on hard were both heading to the damn warzone in Afghanistan and the only thing Trish could do was drop them off for one last night out on the town, and then pray they'd both come home seven long months from now. That pretty much sucked.

~ * ~

Trish pulled along the curb, out of the way of the traffic, and put the car in park.

Crash noticed it was early enough that, unlike when she'd dropped them off this morning just minutes before they were due back onboard, there wasn't a line of cabs and troops streaming toward the boat.

The one good thing about this drive was that Dawn had insisted Zippy sit in the backseat with her. That left Crash in the front next to Trish. It was a small thing, but he felt better being there. Like he wasn't loving her and then leaving her, even though that was exactly what he'd done thanks to Zippy's speedy performance tonight.

He would have thought all that alcohol would have extended the man's stamina. Crash knew from experience that much tequila sure as shit would have meant a marathon session in the bedroom for him. But that wasn't in the cards for tonight.

As Trish cut the engine, Crash opened the door and stepped onto the curb.

83

Trish walked around the car just as Zippy and Dawn crawled from the backseat. "So I guess this is goodbye."

Zippy enveloped Trish in a hug. "I'll call before we leave the country. After that, I'm putting my cell service on hold until we get back."

"Okay. Make sure to email me and give me your mailing address over there so I have it."

"I will."

Trish clung a little tighter before she released Zippy. "Goodbye, big brother."

"Bye, sis. And thanks for the ride."

"You're welcome."

Zippy stepped back and Dawn launched herself at him. While his friend was occupied with a handful of tipsy and now, teary woman, Crash decided to take advantage of the time to say a semi-private goodbye to Trish.

"I had a really good time this weekend."

"Me too." She swallowed hard and raised her gaze to his. "Stay safe, okay?"

"That's the plan." After one more look at Zippy to make sure he was still occupied with Dawn, Crash pulled Trish close and hugged her hard. He'd been inside this woman not even an hour ago. It was a hell of a thing he couldn't even kiss her goodbye now.

Fuck it. Zippy was probably still drunk enough he wouldn't notice anyway. Crash cupped the back of Trish's head, leaned close and pressed his mouth to hers in one brief, hard kiss that he hoped told her how much he did enjoy their time together. All of it.

He pulled back and dropped his hands from her

just as Zippy extricated himself from Dawn's hold.

Zippy turned to Crash. "Ready to go?

"Yup." He dipped his head in a nod and then glanced at Trish. "Thanks again for everything."

"Anytime." So much promise in that one word and her tiny, sad smile, but it was futile. Seven months in Afghanistan was Crash's reality.

"All right. Let's go." Zippy turned and looked both ways, waiting for a break in the traffic to cross the street to get to the club.

Crash hated with everything in him to be leaving to go to a damn club when he and Trish could have had more time together tonight. With a heavy heart, he turned to follow Zippy. Behind him, he heard the doors of Trish's car slam and the engine fire to life.

Their whirlwind weekend fling was good and over. He glanced back long enough to see her pull away from the curb before he had to jog behind Zippy as a car stopped to let them cross.

He'd go to the strip club with his friend. He'd sit there, even have a beer, but Crash knew he'd only be there in body, not in spirit. His mind would be on the woman in that car driving away from him.

CHAPTER EIGHT

Camp Leatherneck/Bastion
Helmand Province, Afghanistan
June 2013

"We have to have a roommate? Seriously?" Zippy turned on the three overhead ceiling lights with a flip of the switch inside the door of their quarters. His lips were pressed together as he shook his head, telling Crash he wasn't done ranting yet. "We're fucking senior staff NCOs, and we don't even get our own quarters on this deployment?"

Crash propped his M4 against the wall just inside the heavy steel door of the windowless, metal Containerized Living Unit he'd call home for the near future.

He made his way across the bare tile floor, leaned against the single table in the CLU and tossed the piece of paper in his hand onto the bare surface next to him. On it was written the five-digit code for the cypher entry lock on their door, but he'd already memorized it.

Crossing his arms, he took in the rest of their accommodations for the next seven months. He eyed the two bunk beds and four mattresses lined up along the walls. Given the set up, he figured they were lucky they only had to double up. One word from command and things could get a whole lot more crowded in their ten by sixteen foot quarters. "You know, most of the other gunnies have four in a can. We should be grateful there's only the two of us in here for now."

"Great." Zippy rolled his eyes. "Keep talking like that and you're gonna jinx us."

"Well, look at it this way. As least we were assigned together. They could have stuck us with some Marines we don't even know." Crash tried to point out the bright side of the situation, though given Zippy's mood right now three strangers as bunkmates might be preferable to his company.

Zippy twisted his mouth to one side. "I guess."

"I heard there's free Wi-Fi. That help any?" If he was going to have to live with him, Crash was determined to knock this shitty attitude out of Zippy.

"I heard it doesn't work more often than it does and the signal is crap." His friend shot him a look and moved toward the bunk beds. "Which side you want?"

"Does it matter?" Crash asked.

Four undecorated steel walls, uninterrupted except for a single door, made up the backdrop of their lush accommodations. It wasn't like there was a view or one side that was better than the other.

"Just asking." Zippy bent to unzip his duffle. "It's freaking freezing in here."

"Well, Jesus, don't bitch about it to anybody. Use a damn blanket and be happy we're not sweltering in this steel box." Given it was about a hundred and eighteen degrees Fahrenheit outside Crash wasn't about to complain the A/C in their can was too cold.

Being raised in the South, Crash firmly believed it was better to be too cold than too hot. A man could always put on more clothes, but he could only take off so many. And he had no intention of sleeping naked with Zippy in the next rack.

"I only brought one blanket with me. I'll see how it is sleeping tonight. I might have to ask Trish or my mom to send me another one."

The mention of Trish caught Crash's attention.

They'd agreed it was a predeployment fling, yet Crash revisited memories of those two nights he'd had with Trish every time his head hit a pillow.

Sometimes when there wasn't even a pillow. He'd thought of her during the layover in Germany while leaning against his bag on the floor of the airport waiting for the next flight. He'd thought of her until he dozed off on the four flights it took to get them from North Carolina to their final destination in the Helmand Province. He had no doubt he'd continue to think of her and the time they spent together while in his rack just feet from her brother.

Boredom. That's what it was that brought his mind to her so often. It's not like there was a television or much else for distraction. Crash hadn't wanted to waste the space in his bags bringing anything to read other than the compact leather-bound bible he'd carried during every deployment he'd been on in his career.

Of course, he'd resort to thinking about Trish. It was a good memory and there was nothing else to think about. That was all it was. It wasn't like he was falling for her or anything.

Still, he couldn't stop himself from extending the conversation. "So, you talk to your family since we left?"

While pawing through clothes in his bag, Zippy said, "Not since we were laid over for those few hours at the base in Maine."

Crash nodded. "I guess we should boot up our laptops and see if there really is usable Wi-Fi. Then we can at least email home to tell them we're safe."

Zippy pulled a set of sheets out of his bag and tossed them on the bed. "I'll try tomorrow. I think we have to get a code to log in anyway. I wanna get unpacked and lie the hell down. I didn't sleep for shit last night in Kyrgyzstan. I'm exhausted. Besides, there's what? An eight and a half hour time difference? Neither Trish or my parents are going to be on Skype right now."

Skype. Crash hadn't thought of that possibility. Email yes, but live video chats, no. While Trish was on with Zippy in their tiny, shared space, Crash would hear her voice. Her image would be just feet from him, in living color on the computer screen.

Shit. So much for his hopes that the memories would fade, that he'd forget about her so he could concentrate on getting through these seven months. This wouldn't help their mutual plan to have a no-strings fling and then part ways.

Strange, but the more Crash thought about it, the more he realized he wasn't all that upset that plan had gone down the crapper. He liked the idea of seeing and hearing her again, even if she was talking to Zippy and not him. Crash couldn't afford an emotional attachment right now, but hell, he could hear her bicker with her brother and enjoy the sound of her laugh without getting attached. Hell, that would be almost as good as having a television.

~ * ~

New Jersey

"Look. I know there's something up with you." Dawn's eyes zeroed in on Trish across the table.

Trish paused, her glass of wine halfway to her mouth. "What? No. What makes you say that?"

"Because the past couple of times we've been out you haven't mentioned our trip to New York once. And if I bring it up you change the subject."

"No, I don't. You're crazy." Trish's heart rate sped. She'd been so careful to not talk about that trip so nothing would slip out about her and Crash, that now Dawn suspected.

"No, I'm not crazy. You're obviously pissed about what happened between your brother and me. I'm sorry, okay? If I'd known it would affect our friendship, I never would have done it. I honestly thought you were behind helping me be with him when you suggested we go up to the room that second night. But I see you weren't and I can't change it now, so can you just please forgive me so we can move on?"

Phew. Trish tried to hold in the breath of relief that threatened to whoosh out of her.

"It's fine. I forgive you." And now Trish had double the guilt to carry around. First, because she was hiding her night with Crash, and more because now Dawn assumed it was the hookup with Danny making things weird between them.

"How's he doing anyway?"

Trish glanced up. "Who?"

"Danny. Your brother. The one in Afghanistan." Dawn's eyes widened as she stared at Trish.

"Oh, he's fine." Christ, she sucked at this lying stuff. "I got an email telling me he's okay and that they'd gotten to Afghanistan. It took them a few days, but they're on base now. They're sharing a room, which they weren't expecting so they're kind of pissed about that."

"They? Who is this *they* you keep talking about?"

And there was one more mistake. Trish had been better off when Dawn thought she was mad. "Danny and Crash. The guy who was here—"

"I remember Crash. He was cute, don't you think?"

Cute was not a word Trish would use to describe Crash. Puppies were cute. Toddlers were cute. Crash was—silent but strong. Big but gentle. Rugged but handsome.

Trish tore herself out of her own thoughts long enough to glance up and see Dawn watching her, brows raised, apparently expecting some sort of response to her last comment. "Uh, yeah. I guess."

Dawn frowned. "Jesus, woman. You need a man. If you're so deep into sexual hibernation you didn't notice that hunka man and how he was looking at you that weekend, we've got an emergency situation here."

"Was he looking at me?" Trish couldn't help it. She had to ask.

"Uh, yes. Oh my God. I'm getting you laid tonight. That's it. Desperate times demand desperate measures." Dawn craned her neck to look around them, presumably for a candidate for her quest to get Trish some sex. Little did Dawn know that Trish had so much sex that first night with Crash, the next day she'd had sore muscles. She'd been sore other places, as well.

There was no way she could be with another guy for a meaningless night of sex now, because what was supposed to be exactly that with Crash, hadn't been meaningless at all. She was clearly incapable of having a one-night stand. She couldn't get him or their parting kiss out of her mind.

Dawn leaned closer. "Okay, there's a guy at the bar. No wedding ring and he keeps glancing this way. I think he's checking us out. You should go flirt with him."

"First of all no wedding ring doesn't mean he's single or available. Second, he's probably checking you out, not me." Trish tipped her head toward the good expanse of cleavage Dawn was showing tonight.

"Yeah, because men never look at you with all that hair of yours bouncing around and those gorgeous green eyes and legs so long you could play women's basketball." Dawn rolled her eyes. "Please."

Trish smiled. "Aw, thanks. You're sweet."

With all the flirting and cleavage, it was sometimes easy to overlook what a genuinely generous person Dawn was.

"Not sweet. It's true." Dawn pushed her chair back from the table and stood. "I'm going to ask if he'd like to join us."

"No!"

Dawn frowned. "Why not?"

"Just please, sit back down."

With a huff, Dawn sat. "What is wrong with you?"

"Nothing. I'm sorry. If you want to talk to him, you go ahead. Just don't bring him over for me, please." Trish remained under Dawn's scrutiny.

"And I'll ask you again, why not? He's cute. He dresses nice. He looks interested. Why don't you want to meet him?"

"Because I had sex with Crash that weekend we were in the city and you were with Danny." The truth came spilling out, and Trish felt the wave of relief wash over her once it had.

It would have come out eventually anyway and everything would be so much easier now that Dawn knew. Not just so Dawn would stop trying to fix her up with random men, but also because Trish needed someone to talk to about what had happened.

"You what?" In her surprise, Dawn's voice was so loud Trish cringed.

"Shh," Trish hissed and kept her own voice low. "You heard me."

"Why didn't you tell me?"

She shrugged. "I don't know. I guess maybe I was embarrassed. I didn't even know him before that weekend."

Dawn dismissed that with a wave of her hand. "So what if you'd just met him? You spent hours together, touring the city, eating, drinking, getting to know each other as well, if not better than you would have if you'd been on a first date."

"I guess."

"I still can't believe you didn't tell me." Dawn put on a scowl, but seemed to get over it as she leaned across the table. "Have you talked to him since? Did he call before he left? Have you been emailing him?"

"No. It was just some fun before he deployed. We agreed on that before we did anything. It wasn't meant to be the start of something." Too bad. Trish wouldn't have minded something. Anything.

"Hmm, I wonder if he's said anything about you to Danny. You could feel your brother out—"

"Oh my God, no. Are you crazy? Danny can't know."

"Trish, they're friends. Why would he care if you're interested in Crash?"

"Because it's not like we agreed to start dating. It was a one-night stand. Well, two nights, but you know what I mean. Danny can't know that."

"You know about Danny and me." Dawn cocked a brow.

"Women are different, I guess. And Crash is different. He's honorable. He didn't want to even consider doing anything because I was his friend's sister. I had to convince him it was okay."

"Convince him, huh? You dirty girl. I never knew you had it in you." A sly smile bowed Dawn's lips.

"Stop. I've been holding this all in with no one to talk to for weeks. Now that you know, I need you to be my friend, not tease me."

"I am your friend. And I don't see a problem."

"You don't?" Trish saw nothing but problems. She'd have to lie to her brother forever about this. And she couldn't stop thinking about Crash.

"Nope. You should be writing to that man. Letters. Emails. Send him dirty pictures of yourself. Whatever. Make his time fly by and when Crash gets back you'll be the first one he wants to see."

Could she? Should she? Trish's cheeks felt hot just thinking about it. "No. I couldn't do that. We didn't even exchange email addresses."

There were some things she could do though. She'd just have to get creative. Trish's mind whirled with the ideas rocketing through her brain. She was aware that Dawn continued to talk, but the words didn't make it through to Trish's consciousness. She didn't wrestle her thoughts back to her friend until Dawn stood.

Trish frowned. "Where are you going?"

"To the bathroom. I just told you that."

"Oh, sorry."

Dawn grabbed her purse. "I sincerely hope if you're going ignore me, it's because you're planning what lingerie to wear for the naughty pictures you're going to send Crash."

Trish rolled her eyes. She couldn't do what Dawn

was suggesting, but she could definitely do something to get Crash's attention. She'd put the plan to work first thing tomorrow morning.

CHAPTER NINE

Camp Leatherneck/Bastion
Helmand Province, Afghanistan
July 2013

The wind whipped hot, dry air and sand at Crash's face. Even in full sunlight, visibility was next to nothing. Crash couldn't see more than a football field away. Not that there was anything to see. Outside the wire, the camp was surrounded by nothing but desolation. Desert as far as the eye could see.

It was eerie knowing the bad guys were out there somewhere. Watching the troop movements. Waiting for an opportunity. All while behind the Hesco barriers life for the troops went on.

Crash picked his way over the rock-strewn ground. It was hard to walk in combat boots, even harder in rubber shoes when he went to the showers each evening. There was nowhere to escape from the damn rocks. They were everywhere, trucked in because even though they made walking difficult in the dry summer, they were necessary for when the rainy season turned the ground to treacherously slick mud.

The rains wouldn't hit until spring when he, God willing, would be home. So for now Crash had to deal with the windstorms and the heat and the rocks. It was well over one hundred degrees today, as usual. Even night didn't bring relief in the summer when the temperature would drop to eighty. That made Crash cross running, even after sunset, off his list of daily PT activities. Yeah, he ran while he was in Djibouti, but he was a few years younger then. Now, he made do with one of the three gyms on base, though only one of those had A/C.

Still, he wouldn't dare complain. How could he in good conscience not be grateful for the amenities they had here? There were troops who had it way worse. He supposed he could deal with the military's rocky solution to the rainy season since they also provided steak, ice cream, and occasionally lobster in the chow hall.

Crash passed the coffee place on his way to his quarters from the barbershop. Church service must have just let out. He saw troops walking, bibles in hand, away from the direction of the chapel. His mother would beat his ass if she knew he hadn't been attending, that after work today he'd chosen to go to the exchange and then get his hair cut.

Working more than twelve hours a day, and then working out at the gym, didn't leave a lot of time to do things like get to the exchange to buy more deodorant when he ran out. Then again, she'd tell him there was always time for God. Crash could hear her voice in his head as clearly as if she were on the phone line for one of their weekly calls.

Maybe next week he'd make time and try to get to a church service.

The bank of stacked CLUs where his quarters were located came into view. Relief from the heat loomed so close Crash picked up speed to get indoors and into the A/C quicker. He punched the code into the lock and swung the reinforced steel door open. The cool air of the can hit him in the face and he breathed deep for the first time since leaving the barbershop to cross the sweltering camp.

As he closed the door against the heat, Crash saw Zippy was already inside. "Hey. What's going on?"

Tearing into a cardboard box, Zippy glanced up. "Care package from home."

"Cool." Crash smothered the envy.

It was ridiculous. He wasn't lacking for anything. Most things he needed he could get at the exchange. If they didn't sell it on base, he could go online and order from a place that would ship to him here.

His mom asked he if needed anything and Crash always told her no. She was getting up there in years and she was on a fixed income. He couldn't expect her to haul packages to the post office when he could order whatever he needed on his own. But there was something about getting a little piece of home at mail call that made a guy feel good.

He sat on his rack and glanced over. "What'd you get?"

"All sorts of shit. It's like Trish bought out the store." Zippy pawed through the sizable box.

Trish. That piqued Crash's interest in the box further. "Yeah? Anything good?" Christ, that had sounded a little too interested.

Zippy starting unloading the contents onto the desk. "Peanut butter. Crackers. A couple of DVDs. Box of cookies."

"Oh, that's nice." The cloud of disappointment darkened over Crash.

"Here." Zippy turned and tossed a smaller box toward Crash.

As it came sailing across the room, Crash reached out and caught it between his fingertips. "What's this?"

"I don't know. Open it. It's got your name on it."

His eyes widened when he turned the box in his hands and saw it did indeed have his name written on it in bold black marker. CRASH. Nothing else, but he knew who it had to be from.

"Trish sent me something?"

"I guess so." Zippy didn't look surprised or suspicious. He was too busy tearing through the rest of the box.

If Zippy wasn't concerned that Trish was sending Crash things, then Crash figured he needn't worry. He couldn't beat down the excitement as he tore the packing tape off and opened the flaps of the cardboard box. He smiled at what he saw on top. A note, in handwriting he didn't recognize because they'd never written to each other before. Strange that he knew the feel, the taste, the scent of this girl, but had never seen her writing until now.

Crash.

I remembered you said you liked these so I thought I'd send some along. FYI, don't know how you can eat that stuff!

Trish

He peered into the box and found half a dozen cans of sardines, a box of crackers and a bag of beef jerky. His favorite snacks on earth. They'd talked about food that weekend they were together. He remembered she'd made the funniest face when he mentioned the sardines. He'd teased her because she'd never even tried one, but had already decided she hated them.

His heart clenched as he tried not to make more of it than there was. She'd been sending stuff to her brother. She'd probably just thrown this in as an afterthought.

The falseness of his rationalization echoed through him. Trish had remembered their conversation. She'd taken the time to search out and find exactly the things she knew he liked. This was no afterthought.

"That was real nice of Trish. If you're on with her later and I'm not here, tell her thanks from me."

Zippy had a habit of logging into Skype while Crash was at the gym. Or sometimes while Crash ate at the chow hall, Zippy would come back to the can for a nap or to call home on the computer. Crash had been in the room only once while Zippy had been online with Trish, but even that brief glimpse of her on the monitor and the sound of her voice had brought back vivid memories of that weekend.

"All right. Will do." Zippy's flip answer didn't seem like enough. Besides the fact Crash didn't trust him to remember.

Crash wanted to thank this amazing woman properly. "You know what, give me her email so I can say thanks myself."

"Okay. Whatever." Zippy shrugged. "Remind me later when I'm online and I'll shoot you her email address."

"A'ight." Crash blew out a breath. The deception was starting to wear on him.

Otherwise occupied, Zippy didn't seem suspicious at all. That was good, because as he peeked inside his box again at the odd assortment of things she'd sent him, and then at the note on the mattress next to him, Crash couldn't help his goofy grin.

CHAPTER TEN

Camp Leatherneck/Bastion
Helmand Province, Afghanistan
August 2013

Crash pushed through the door of his CLU mid morning to find Zippy on the computer for his usual lunchtime break.

Guiltily, Crash glanced at the screen to see if Zippy was online with his sister. Crash and Trish had exchanged a few casual emails over the past few weeks. Him thanking her. Her responding and asking how he was. Him replying.

Nothing serious, nothing much, but enough contact to keep her uppermost in his mind. Enough to make the off chance he'd get to see her on video on Zippy's computer screen enticing.

No such luck today. Trish's pretty smile wasn't on the computer. Instead, some ugly dead guy stumbled his decaying corpse across the screen. Zippy was watching that television show he liked so much. Something about zombies. The man had gone insane when he realized the Wi-Fi in the cans wasn't strong enough to stream video. Thank God the tech guy here had managed to get this season saved on an external hard drive. It might have been the only thing that prevented Crash from strangling Zippy to stop his incessant ranting about missing the new episodes.

Zippy hit pause and glanced over his shoulder as Crash walked across the CLU toward his rack. "Did you see the email that came through this morning?"

"The one from the Maintenance Chief about keeping our weapons close? Yeah. That's why I'm carrying that thing again." Crash tipped his head toward the M4 he'd leaned against the wall just inside the door when he'd walked in.

General orders specified that they carry a weapon at all times on Leatherneck/Bastion, but the week they'd gotten there his OIC, Captain Lee, had told Crash just carrying his pistol was enough and he could lock up the semi-automatic rifle. Today, after receiving that ominous email that troops were to not only carry their weapons but also make sure to keep them close, Crash had gotten the M4 back out. Why the change, he wasn't sure.

"What do you think is up?" Crash asked.

"Who the hell knows? There must have been some sort of a threat. I swear, the way the press is nowadays, Trish gets more information at home than we get from the command, and we're the ones freaking here." Zippy frowned at Crash. "What are you doing?"

"My mom emailed. It's my aunt's birthday next week and I forgot. I gotta send her a card."

"Next week?" Zippy cocked a brow. "It's not gonna make it in time."

"Nope. Probably not, but at least I can say I tried." He was in friggin' Afghanistan. His aunt would just have to understand.

Crash pulled his address book out from the drawer of the rolling plastic storage unit the last inhabitant of this CLU had left for them when he'd shipped out. It was one of the better things they'd discovered upon moving in.

They'd also inherited a bunch of cans of protein powder from the last occupant, but a few doses of that had taught them that all it did was give them gas. Two guys in a tiny confined space, both farting up a storm thanks to some body building powder, was not worth whatever muscles it was supposed to give them. He'd dumped the rest of the cans on the shelves at work for the other guys to take if they wanted.

Having gotten what he'd come for, the book containing his aunt's address, Crash grabbed his weapon and glanced at Zippy. "You going back soon?"

"In a bit. I just want to finish this episode."

"A'ight." Crash shook his head at Zippy's taste in television and headed back out into the glaring sunlight, across the annoying rocks and into the steel headquarters building where he worked twelve, sometimes thirteen hours a day.

The Master Sergeant glanced up as Crash walked

in. "We just got word from the Maintenance Chief."

"Yeah, I saw the email."

"No, not that one. A runner came by to pass new word. Apparently the Chief just had a meeting."

That news piqued Crash's interest. Here might be an explanation about the reason for the heightened security. "Yeah?"

"He reemphasized about the weapons. To not just have them with us, but to keep them at arm's length at all times."

Arm's length at all times. That meant Crash would have to sleep with the M4 next to his rack rather than by the door, and he'd need to figure out how to take his pistol into the shower with him. Lovely. "That all?"

"Nope. There's more good news." The sarcasm was clear in the Master Sergeant's tone. "We're all going to have to take roving duty after work. The shift runs from eighteen hundred to twenty-one hundred hours. I worked it out. There are enough of us we'll only have to do it twice a month to cover all the slots."

Jesus, now they had senior staff pulling guard duty? What the hell was going on? "Any hint as to why?"

"No, but maybe we'll hear that in the meeting."

"What meeting?" Crash had left for less than an hour to eat lunch in the chow hall and run by his can, and it seemed he'd missed all sorts of shit.

"Check your email."

Sighing, Crash sat and logged into his computer. Sure enough, there was an email in his inbox. They'd called a senior staff NCO meeting starting in—he glanced at the time in the corner of the screen—half an hour. At least maybe they'd finally hear what was up.

~ * ~

"No eating in the chow hall. You get your food and leave. No gathering in large groups of any kind." The Senior Enlisted Advisor, Master Gunnery Sergeant Devon, passed on that order to the stunned Marines in the room. "Direct order from the CO, Lieutenant Colonel Hinman."

Crash and close to two dozen senior staff NCOs, including Zippy, sat around the long table in the large conference room located across the hall from where Crash worked in Production Control. There were two large TVs and a big-eye for doing computer generated power point presentations, but it seemed they wouldn't be needing any of that for this meeting.

No more chow hall. Senior enlisted on roving guard duty. Weapons at arm's length, even in quarters. "What the hell is going on?"

Crash had whispered the question more to himself than to anyone else, but the guy next to him leaned close. "Ramadan's ending. They're afraid that's when the shit's gonna hit the fan."

Shit was a good word right about now.

CHAPTER ELEVEN

A week in, the no eating in the chow hall order was starting to wear on him. Crash barely took a lunch break any more. He'd get his food, bring it back to his office and eat at his desk. That made his twelve plus hour day seem to drag by even slower than usual.

Maybe he should start going back to the CLU and take his lunch breaks there with Zippy, but that would mean watching one of Zippy's weird ass TV shows.

Nope, better to stay in the office.

Crash swallowed a forkful of tuna and glanced at his screen as his email alert chimed. He smiled as a message from Trish popped into his inbox and clicked to open it.

Just checking in. You need more sardines yet? (Ick!)

Hope you're having a good day!

Trish

She was so damn cute. He hit reply and had just laid his hands on the keyboard to write a message back when, for no apparent reason, he lost signal.

Now what? He truly didn't understand how they could have such shitty internet on a major base in this day and age. He sat and waited, hoping it was just a blip and the signal would come back. The warning flashing across his screen told him this was no blip and this was no run of the mill internet outage.

The code word that crossed his screen told Crash command had cut all communications for everything coming from or going to anywhere other than Leatherneck/Bastion. This was not good.

Exterior communications were intentionally blocked for a number of reasons. Death of a military member, a visiting dignitary or high-dollar general, or an attack—either against the allies or initiated by them.

What had prompted this one? He hated to think it was a casualty. It had been so quiet lately he'd thought the precautions put in place by command for the possible attacks at the end of Ramadan had been insane. The holiday had ended yesterday at sunset, but nothing had happened last night, when Crash had assumed any attack would have come.

The sound of the base-wide alarm told Crash this was no visiting dignitary. This was an attack. The insurgents had been biding their time, or maybe celebrating yesterday, but now they were ready to fight.

He stood fast, sending his desk chair skidding

behind him as he did. Crash grabbed his body armor and turned to the other personnel in the office. "Flaks and Kevlars on."

Pistol in his holster and his rifle in hand, he headed out of the office door and peered inside to the room next to his. "What's happening?"

The Marine inside in the process of pulling on his own Flak shook his head. "Hell if I know."

With an uneasy feeling in his stomach, Crash moved farther down the hall as the alarms continued to sound. He neared the closed door of the CO's office and could hear the muffled conversation of the commander and the Executive Officer, Major Hintner, inside.

Eavesdropping was not usually Crash's thing, but this was not a usual situation. He leaned closer hoping to hear something, anything, positive.

He jumped as the door swung wide. The XO stood in the opening glaring at Crash, who couldn't hide he'd been listening. Whatever was happening had the Major pushing past him and heading toward the Maintenance Chief's office rather than reprimanding Crash.

This had to be bad.

Pushing his luck a bit further, Crash followed. He arrived in time to hear most of the XO's conversation with the Maintenance Chief.

"—get word out to every division chief to have all Marines don their Flaks and Kevlars and have all firearms at the ready, condition three."

The weapons were to remain in condition three—bolt forward, full magazine in, weapon on safe. It still didn't tell Crash why or what had happened.

"Roger that." The sound of the Maintenance Chief's chair scraping across the floor had Crash jumping back from the door and slipping into his own office before he could be seen again. He'd been caught once already. Attack or no, that was enough for one day.

The Master Sergeant in Crash's office, weapon in hand as he watched his computer screen, glanced up when Crash slipped in. "You find out what happened?"

"No. You?" Crash asked.

"No."

Crash heard the Maintenance Chief barking at some Marines out in the hallway. It sounded as if he was grabbing them to act as runners to get the word out to Marines not near their computers. Three for the detached maintenance shops, and three more for the CLUs where the personnel working night crew would be sleeping. But the Chief pulled the six into his office before Crash could hear what that word they'd be passing was.

An email alert chimed on the Master Sergeant's and Crash's computers simultaneously. Crash moved to his desk and bent low to read it. It was an all hands internal communication from the Maintenance Chief repeating the same orders he'd overheard the XO give while he'd been listening, plus the order that they were to report immediately to the nearest bunker and remain there for accountability checks.

Still no explanation as to why. Crash couldn't take it anymore. He strode into the hall and found the Maintenance Chief in his office in front of his computer, which made sense since he'd just sent that email.

"Excuse me, Master Sergeant. What's happened?"

The man glanced up, the severity of the situation clearly visible on his face. "The main gate on Leatherneck was compromised."

"By who?"

"Not exactly sure. The suicide vest detonated before we could ask him."

Fuck. No other words came to mind as Crash stood dumbstruck.

"Get to a bunker, Gunnery Sergeant."

"Roger that, Top." On autopilot, Crash made his way outside as ordered.

"Did you fucking hear what happened?" Zippy's question knocked Crash out of his daze the moment he got inside the bunker.

"Suicide bomber breached the gate on Leatherneck. That's all I know." Six miles away from where they were on Bastion. No wonder he hadn't heard the explosion.

"Yeah, but there's more. There were casualties."

Crash's attention snapped to Zippy. "How many?"

"Don't know, but multiple. I heard there were both Brits and Americans killed."

"Fuck."

"Yeah. And I heard we intercepted some messages. In between the praying, the enemy is ranting about fire raining down from the sky to take out all infidels."

Heightened adrenaline had Crash's mouth dry and his hand tightening on his weapon.

An explosion sounded in the distance, but still too close for comfort. Crash turned to Zippy. "There's that fire from the sky you heard about."

A Corporal ran into the bunker, his face white. "A rocket just hit the flightline. It destroyed at least one of the Ospreys."

This was no single suicide bomber. This was a coordinated attack and they were targeting the aircraft.

The indirect fire warning sirens sounded as more Marines pushed into the bunkers located next to the HQ building. As the rockets continued to explode around them, they had no other choice but to hunker down and wait. Wait for new orders. Wait for the attack to end. The problem was, Crash wasn't real good at waiting.

The bunker, already like an oven, became filled with Marines and the stench of sweat and fear. It was almost unbearably hot, but there was nothing they could do about it besides look forward to the coming sunset. Then at least it would cool off a little. But that was a double-edged sword considering what was going on. If the enemy was this bold in broad daylight, what the hell did they have planned for when night hit?

"What should we do, Gunnery Sergeant?"

At that question from a Corporal, Crash glanced around and realized he and Zippy were the two senior Marines in the bunker.

"We stay put," Zippy answered the younger Marine.

Crash had heard stories about the rocket attacks that had plagued this area since the camps were built. Likely every Marine in this bunker had heard them too. The attacks came from out of the blue, but didn't last long. As soon as a hunter-killer team, the Huey and a Cobra helicopter sections that flew together, was able to launch, they would find the source of the rockets and destroy it. Then all would be right with the world again—until the next insurgents found their way through the desert and within range of the camp.

But today's attack had targeted the flightline, possibly damaging the aircraft for their close air support, and Crash didn't know how long it would be before the good guys could launch an air attack, if they were able to at all.

The rockets continued, giving no indication that they'd stop any time soon. The Marines stayed put, as ordered. Some cussed, some prayed, some were silent. Most were young maintainers on their first deployment, not sure that they had made the right choice to come in the military amidst a twelve-year war. Unlike Crash, they would have been children during the attacks of nine-eleven and when this war started.

Crash pulled the small notebook he always kept on him out of his pocket along with a pen. He'd have to jot down the names of everyone in the bunker, starting with those standing nearest to him. He'd need that information for the accountability muster that someone would be calling for as soon as the attack subsided.

Nearby, one young female Marine was visibly

shaken. Tears ran down her cheeks as she clutched her rifle.

"Crap." Crash didn't need hysterics in the middle of an attack, and this young Marine didn't need the reputation having a breakdown right now would give her. It would follow her for the rest of her career.

Zippy followed Crash's gaze and saw her too. "I'll handle it." He took a step closer to her. "Where you from, Corporal?"

"Phoenix." Her voice trembled.

"Well then, you must be used to this kind of heat, huh?"

"Yes, Gunny."

"But it's a dry kind of heat, right?" Zippy asked, humor in his voice. "Isn't that what you Arizona people always say?"

He got a small, shaky smile out of the girl. "Yes, Gunny."

Crash heard the low murmur of Zip's voice, followed by hers while the conversation continued and Zip did his best to calm, or at least distract her so the others wouldn't see how badly she was affected by the attack. Just talking to her seemed to help. With Zippy on that duty, Crash moved through the bunker to get the rest of the names.

As the sun slipped over the horizon, darkness fell and the sounds of the explosions subsided. Still, they stayed put. Like it or not, they couldn't leave the bunker until the all clear alarm sounded.

There was a variety of reactions to their forced confinement. Some rested easy. One guy even managed to sleep while sitting propped against the wall. Most remained vigilant, especially the senior Marines, Zippy and Crash among them.

Crash wasn't about to let his guard down. He'd heard stories about how the insurgents would fire the rockets in bursts, sometimes thirty minutes to an hour apart.

It was close to half an hour of silence when the sound of another rocket exploded in the vicinity of the flightline, followed by a second.

So much for the peace and quiet and so much for launching an air attack. Who knew what shape the aircraft were in at this point?

Another rocket whistled through the air, the sound coming in their direction almost in slow motion before it impacted between the bunker where they were and another one some hundred feet away. The blast caused the ten-inch thick concrete bunker's heavy top to shift, putting them all inside at risk of being crushed to death. Crash for one, was not about to sit in that death trap and wait for the roof to fall on him.

"We gotta get them the hell out of here." Crash spoke low enough only Zippy would be able to hear.

"Agreed."

Crash moved to the entrance and peered outside, searching for the telltale trail of another rocket. Seeing no sign of any, he turned back to the Marines inside the bunker. "This roof's not safe. Split up and get into the bunkers nearby."

The occupants scattered on his command, leaving Crash and Zippy alone just as another rocket impacted close by again, causing the bunker top to groan and scrape as it shifted even more on top of the supports. The blast rocked the ground so hard, Crash had to reach for the wall to keep his balance.

"Fuck. We can't stay here and those other bunkers are already overflowing." Zip glanced at Crash.

"I know." More than that, Crash wasn't so keen on crowded, confined spaces. Particularly those with a concrete roof that could, with one well-placed blast, be knocked off the two parallel walls it rested precariously upon.

"You wanna try for the berm?" Zippy asked, probably thinking the same thing as Crash, better to be outside than in here crushed under a ton of concrete.

"A'ight. Let's go."

Knowing the troops they'd been with were now under the care of the senior guys in the other bunkers, Crash followed Zippy. They raced towards a dirt and gravel berm and hit the sand. Crash spun to face the direction of the rocket attack.

"Now what?" Zippy asked, his eyes on the perimeter fencing.

Crash adjusted the position of his rifle and stared in the same direction, feeling moderately better that if anyone tried to breach the wire, at least from here he could do something about it.

"I guess we wait for the all clear."

Or for the bad guys to run out of rockets.

Or for air support to get off the ground, if it ever did.

Until then, Crash's hands would remain on his

weapon and his eyes on the perimeter. There wasn't much else he could do, except maybe pray.

CHAPTER TWELVE

New Jersey

Trish hadn't heard back from Danny or Crash, when usually both of them would reply to her. She'd installed a world clock on her computer and knew exactly what time it was on their base and what hours they worked. If she emailed during their day, they'd always get right back to her. At least within the hour, because she knew sometimes they'd take a break for meals or have a meeting.

But not yesterday. She'd emailed the moment she'd woken up in the morning, when it was still afternoon for Crash and Danny. Then she'd heard nothing. When it got to be her night, which meant it was their morning, she'd sat up and waited until eleven before she'd given up and gone to bed. They should have been at their desk for hours by then, but neither had emailed.

Trish had fallen to sleep eventually, but now, at four in the morning, she was awake again and worrying. To hell with it. Staying in bed wide awake was an exercise in frustration. She wasn't going to be able rest until she checked her email, so she got up and booted up the computer. When that took too long, she grabbed her cell phone and hit the email icon.

Scrolling through her inbox, her heart clenched when there was nothing from either of them.

"Okay. That doesn't mean anything. Maybe the internet is out. My internet goes out and I'm not even in Afghanistan." Who she was talking to, she had no idea. She didn't even have a cat.

Trish tossed her cell on the counter and headed for the coffee maker. There'd be no more sleep for her until she'd heard something. That was fine. Today was Saturday. She didn't have to be at work until Monday morning. She could sit here all day and all night, and then all day again tomorrow.

Jesus, she hoped she heard from them before tomorrow. She didn't think she'd be able to take worrying for that long.

The pot of coffee, consumed on an empty stomach, only put Trish more on edge. When the phone finally rang mid morning, she jumped from the sound. Dawn's name appeared in the readout and Trish forced herself to take a breath. Jittery from the caffeine, her hands shook as she hit the button to answer.

"Good morning." Dawn's cheery greeting didn't brighten Trish's mood any, not that that was her friend's fault.

"Hey."

"What's wrong?"

Trish should have known she wouldn't be able to hide anything from Dawn. "I haven't heard from Danny or Crash in days."

"Okay, is that normal?"

"No, they always respond to me."

"So you have been writing to Crash—"

"Dawn, this is not the time."

"All right. Let's think this out. Could they be busy on a mission or something?"

Trish realized how little she knew about the job her brother performed for the military. "I don't think so. He's never disappeared for days before."

"Wouldn't your parents have been notified if anything bad happened?"

"Yeah."

"Then there's nothing to worry about."

"You're right. The internet is probably broken."

"There you go. That's got to be it. My internet went out for like twenty minutes last night. Thought I'd lose my mind."

Trish smiled. Nothing like Dawn's insanity to provide a distraction. She was about to suggest Dawn come over for lunch and distract her further when the call waiting beeped in. Trish pulled the phone away from her face to glance at the caller ID.

The unknown number listed as originating in Maryland had her heart clenching. Who was this? Unsolicited sales calls didn't come through to her cell phone. They only plagued her on the home line. There was a lot of military in Maryland. This could be a call about Danny.

"Oh my God."

"What? What's happening?" Dawn's frantic question told Trish she'd spoken aloud.

"There's a call coming through from Maryland."

"Well, answer it! And call me right back."

"Okay. Bye." Her nerves didn't help the shaking as she rushed to answer the call she wasn't sure she wanted to get. "Hello?"

"Trish?"

"Yes."

"It's Crash."

She grabbed the edge of the table as the room swayed. "What's wrong? Has something happened to Danny?"

"Oh, no. Crap. I didn't even think you'd assume anything . . . Trish, I just saw Zippy, He's fine. I swear."

"Okay." She let out a shaky breath. "I'm sorry I jumped on you. It's just when I didn't hear back from either of you—"

"I know. Comm was down. It's back up now. I'll tell Zippy to contact you."

"Thanks." She lowered herself into a chair and tried to calm herself.

"I really am sorry I scared you."

"It's okay." Now that she knew her brother wasn't dead or injured, and her heart wasn't pounding hard enough to have her feeling dizzy, she could appreciate the deep tenor of Crash's voice funneled directly into her ear through the phone. His soft Southern drawl washed over her and brought back vivid memories of their weekend. Crash calling her still seemed odd, but wonderful.

Something else was odd, as well. "The caller ID said Maryland . . ."

"Yeah, they route our calls through the States."

"Oh. I didn't even realize you have phones there. Danny always just emails or Skypes me."

"Yeah, we have a call center set up here, but you need a calling card."

"Oh." Even more intriguing. Crash had not only taken the time to phone her, but he'd had to use a calling card to do it. "So how are you?"

"Good. We had a little, uh, excitement around here, but I'm good. Zippy is too. Um, that's kind of what I wanted to talk to you about."

"Your excitement or my brother?" It seemed Crash's answers only raised more questions, but Trish was more than willing to take the time to figure out the mystery of this man.

His laugh came through her cell. "Both, I guess. I had some time to think the other night, and I talked to Zippy. Anyway, long story short, I told him about us. About that weekend. And I know I should have talked to you first, but there were extenuating circumstances."

"Okay. I trust you. If you thought you needed to tell him, that's fine."

"You trust me?"

She smiled at the happiness she heard in his voice. "Yes, of course I do."

"I'm glad."

"So, uh, how'd Danny take the news of our little fling?"

"He wasn't happy about it, but he never beat the crap out of me the way he said he was going to so that's something, I guess."

Trish laughed. "That's good. I'm glad to hear it. Is he the one who gave you my phone number?"

"No, actually, he'd called you from my phone that one time. My service is cut off but the phone still had the outgoing call log in it. I'm sorry, it's probably out of line for me to just call—"

"No, not at all. It's fine. Really." Trish smiled. She'd made love to this man three times over the course of two days, and he was worried he'd taken liberties by calling her? Southern men really were a different breed. Different, but nice.

"Okay. I'm glad you don't mind." He dragged in a breath. "So the reason I'm calling . . . you know how we said that weekend was just for fun, and that it wouldn't mean anything later on?"

"Yeah."

"Well, what if I changed my mind about that? I think it did mean something. And I think we should take some time to get to know each other better, and see if we can make it work. At least, I want it to try, *if* that's what you want."

Now it was no longer fear that had Trish's heart pounding. "Yeah, I'd like that."

"Good." He let out a loud breath. "That's real good. But I gotta warn you, life as a Marine girlfriend isn't easy."

Hearing him use the word *girlfriend* in relation to her being with him sent a thrill through her. "That's okay. We Jersey girls are pretty tough. I can handle it."

"I'm very happy to hear that. So, um, now that we've talked, maybe I can Skype you sometime?"

"Definitely." She felt like a schoolgirl. Like the quarterback had just asked her to the prom. Giddy. Excited. Nervous. Unable to stop smiling. It was too much to absorb all at once and she loved every bit of it.

"A'ight. Good. So I'll be talking to you then. And I'll email you too."

"Okay." Warmth spread through Trish just from the promise of hearing from him.

"I better get going before this phone card runs out and cuts us off."

"Um, Crash. Can I ask you something real quick before you hang up?"

"Sure. Shoot."

"How'd you get your nickname?"

He chuckled. "I was afraid that would come up. It's kind of an embarrassing story, but here it goes— I backed a jeep into a building during Marine Combat Training. Been called Crash ever since."

Trish smiled. "Thanks for sharing."

"You're welcome. Now, I really better go. Bye for now?"

She bit her lip at his sweetness. "Bye for now."

The line went dead and Trish lowered the phone.

What a difference five minutes could make. She had to call Dawn back and tell her everything was okay. More than okay. Trish had to tell her the crazy but incredible news about her and Crash. She just wasn't sure she'd be able to make the call. She was still shaking, but it had nothing to do with the coffee.

~ * ~

Crash couldn't help the goofy smile on his face

125

as he pushed through the door of his CLU, but he tried to control it for Zippy's sake. "Hey."

"Hey." Zippy responded without looking up from his computer screen and the TV show playing there.

Crash glanced at his friend's back from across the can. "You still mad at me?"

Still not making eye contact, Zippy said, "I'm deciding."

"A'ight. Fair enough. While you're deciding, I wanted you to know I called Trish."

That got Zippy's attention. He paused the show and turned in his chair. "You what?"

"I called her from the phone center."

"Why?" The wariness in Zippy's tone told Crash he wasn't out of the woods with his friend yet.

"Because I like her, Zip. A lot. I wanna get to know her better. And then, when we're home, I wanna see her."

"So you didn't just want to fuck her then?"

"Jesus, Zip." Crash set his jaw. Yeah, he'd been in the wrong doing what he'd done with Trish behind Zippy's back, but Zippy had no right to talk like that about a lady, especially his own sister. "Please don't say that word again in relation to Trish."

Zippy's brow's rose. "Fine. You two do whatever you want to do. It's her life."

Not exactly a blessing, but at least no blows had been exchanged. For now, that would have to be good enough.

"Thanks." Crash turned to leave.

He'd finished his workday and gone directly to the phone center. Now that the nerve-wracking phone call was over, he was starving. He could grab something, bring it back to his desk and log into email. Send Trish a nice long message. He liked that idea.

"I'm hitting the gym in about an hour. Wanna come?" Zippy's question stopped Crash with his hand on the doorknob.

"Yeah, sure."

"Okay. See you there." Zip turned back to his computer and hit play on the show again.

"A'ight." Maybe things were good between them after all.

A few minutes later, armed with a take out container from the chow hall, Crash was back at his office, but this time, not to work. He leaned his weapon against the wall behind him and sat.

While chewing on a big mouthful of tuna salad sandwich, he logged into is email and saw a name from the past sitting in his inbox. His old friend Beau. Crash hadn't seen him in close to a year. That's what happened when a guy got married, he guessed. It was hard to get out with friends. Add to that the double whammy of Beau being in another squadron now on another base and they didn't cross paths too often.

It was still good to hear from an old friend now. Crash took another bite and clicked to open the email.

To: O'Malley GSgt John
From: Adams GSgt Beau
Hey, Crash,
I've got some news for you. Since you were there from the very beginning, and you were my best man,

I wanted you to be the first to know that Carrie's pregnant. I couldn't be happier. She's real excited too, except when the morning sickness had her ralphing while she was up in the bird. Don't tell her I told you that!

Otherwise, things are status quo here in Cherry Point. What's up with you? How's summer in sunny Afghanistan? Can't say I envy you being there. I still remember the heat in Djibouti too well. Though, I'll admit, I am pissed you'll have the Afghanistan campaign medal and I won't.

Say hey to Zippy for me. I'm gonna have to shoot him an email as well.

Catch ya later,

Beau

Crash smiled. His buddy Beau was going to be a father. He was happy for him and his wife. They'd had a long haul in the beginning with them both being military and deployed when they'd met, but it had all worked out in the end.

Their relationship should have been a lesson to Crash. Even when the obstacles looked insurmountable, things could work. He realized that now though.

After the entire base had been pinned down by the enemy for hours during the attack, little things such as being separated for a few more months from Trish seemed like nothing. Piece of cake. Even the distance between New Jersey and North Carolina seemed manageable. Where there was a will, there was a way. When he got back they'd see about making it work. That was definitely something to look forward to.

Smiling just thinking about being home and on the same continent as Trish again, Crash hit reply and started to type.

Hey, Beau.

Congrats! Great news about the baby. Send Carrie my love.

Yeah, hot as hell here, in more ways than one if you get my meaning, but you, me and Zip can talk about that over a beer when we get back in January.

So, I do have some news of my own. I've met someone. She's amazing! And you're not going to believe whose sister she is . . .

If you've enjoyed Cinderella Liberty *please consider leaving a review and don't miss Beau and Carrie's story in* Crossing the Line.

Look for Cat's other military romances including the USA Today bestselling Hot SEALs series.

Hot SEALs

Night with a SEAL
Saved by a SEAL
SEALed at Midnight
Kissed by a SEAL
Protected by a SEAL
Loved by a SEAL
Tempted by a SEAL
Wed to a SEAL
Romanced by a SEAL
Rescued by a Hot SEAL

For more titles visit CatJohnson.net

ABOUT THE AUTHOR

Cat Johnson is a top 10 *New York Times* bestseller and the author of the *USA Today* bestselling Hot SEALs series. She writes contemporary romance featuring sexy alpha heroes and is known for her unique marketing. She has sponsored pro bull riders, owns a collection of camouflage and western wear for book signings, and has used bologna to promote romance novels. A fair number of her book consultants wear combat or cowboy boots for a living.

Never miss a new release or a sale again.
Join Cat's inner circle at catjohnson.net/news

Made in the USA
San Bernardino, CA
23 August 2016